WATER & POWER

WATER & POWER
A NOVEL BY
STEVEN DUNN

TARPAULIN SKY PRESS
CA ∴ CO ∴ NY ∴ VT
2018

10% of author proceeds will be donated to the International
Refugee Committee. www.rescue.org

Cover photo by Jay Halsey.

Tarpaulin Sky Press
P.O. Box 189
Grafton, Vermont 05146
TarpaulinSky.com

For more information on Tarpaulin Sky Press trade paperback
and hand-bound editions, as well as information regarding dis-
tribution, personal orders, and catalogue requests, please visit our
website at tarpaulinsky.com.

for

Anwar Belt	DeShawn Crawford
Felix Hamm	Robert Burris
Lorenzo James	Anthony Walker
Kevin Wright	Michael Echols
Isaiah Baggett	Chris Mudd
Nico Figueroa	Antonio Dixon
Carlton Jakes	Ace Williams
Nyesha Henderson	William Henderson

Chapter Q & Some A

umbrella swell of jellyfish. muffled voices. plastic bottle
bobs weightless wavy arms, wrinkled fingerprints. air blobs
burst at surface   no trace of submersion

In *FABRIC*, Richard Froude says that submersion means:
One field's absolute disappearance within another.

I am interested in the submersion of individuals within the
military. I am also interested in the breach.

Q: How do you write about something so large, but
   largely invisible?
A: Something that large must have cracks.
Q: Write from the cracks?
A:
Q: Climb down feet first or headfirst?
A:

Preface

So, from the cracks, I tried to write an Ethnography [from Greek *ethno*, "folk, people, nation," and *graph*, "to write"]. Ethnography is research designed to explore cultural phenomena.

I conducted this research for 10 years. I asked military members a few questions. Mostly I said, "Tell me something about your experience." Sometimes they did. Most Subjects insisted that no one could possibly understand until they've served in the military themselves. I don't claim to understand.

I sat in the swirl with spread fingers and gathered the filaments.

Data Collection (Filaments):
Sources include but are not limited to: Subject Interviews and my own Participation, Observation, Military Documents, Brief Histories, and Field Notes. A resulting Case Report will reflect the knowledge and the systems of meanings in the lives of this particular cultural group.

Participation

Raise your right hand and repeat after me.

I, _____, do solemnly swear that I will support and defend the Constitution of the United States against all enemies, foreign and domestic . . .

I, _____, do solemnly swear that I will support and defend the Constitution of the United States against all enemies, foreign and domestic . . .

. . . that I will bear true faith and allegiance to the same . . .

. . . that I will bear true faith and allegiance to the same . . .

. . . and that I will obey the orders of the President of the United States . . .

. . . and that I will obey the orders of the President of the United States . . .

. . . and the orders of the officers appointed over me . . .

. . . and the orders of the officers appointed over me . . .

. . . according to regulations and the Uniform Code of Military Justice.

. . . according to regulations and the Uniform Code of Military Justice.

. . . So help me God.

. . . So help me God.

Welcome to my boot camp, shipmates. Oh, look at you three cuties. Can't be separated, huh? What corner of this great nation did you all crawl from?

West Virginia.

Black people in West Virginia? I'm surprised you all have teeth. Do you like fucking your sisters?

No.

You know the best way to castrate a man from West Virginia?

No.

Kick his sister in the jaw.

Boot camp ain't too bad.
Boot camp ain't too bad.
Boot camp ain't too bad.

I can't sleep. The guy above me is snoring. So is the guy next to me. The guy above him is jacking off, that scratchy grey blanket is going up and down up and down. I close my eyes tight and say, I'm doing something important, I'm doing something important, I'm doing something important. I get up to go pee. I walk in the head. A guy is trying to slit his wrist, disposable razor blood on sink. He sees me in the mirror. Oh, I say. That's okay, he says, shitty razors.

Too many of us are joking around or trying to kill ourselves or getting homesick or getting fed up. With what, we do not know.

But our RDC (Recruit Division Commander) says that we do not have appreciation. For what, we do not know.

So he corrals us into the concrete courtyard and tells us to stand at attention until he returns. On the top of the barracks, in each corner, large speakers play that one song.

Our RDC returns, with the triangle folded flag cradled to his chest. At ease, he says. He instructs us to gather around the flag and touch it. The song swells, *God Bless the USAAAAAA.* They start crying.

Field Notes

Before the first interview I asked one of the subjects, "Can I trust you tell the truth?"

She said, "Can I trust *you* to tell the truth?"

"Um, I don't know what I'm telling the truth about."

"Me either," she said.

Subject Interview #00012

Man, that shit that happened in New York changed a lot of stuff: People's mindsets, the reasons why people joined, all types of stuff. Especially the security to get on base. Before that, I was able to bring civilian girls back to my barracks room all willy-nilly.

I was at the club with this chick . . . drinking, dancing, everything. She wanted to go back to my spot cuz her place was too far. It started out as a half-serious joke, you know. I told her, "You can get in the trunk." I didn't think she'd agree. But she got in. I told her not to make any noise. Security checked under the car for bombs, they even knocked on the trunk. Luckily, we made it smooth through. They would've thought we were terrorists or something.

Observation

I have to go to medical because I think I have a bladder infection. It might be an STD.

In the waiting room, Osama Bin Laden is on the news again, hiking again. He looks happy. His gray beard is long and flowing. And his staff looks sturdy.

On the table is a copy of *The Army Times*. Osama Bin Laden's face is on the front, like he went to the state fair and got himself drawn with thick black markers.

I have to pee every five minutes.

The news says that those mountains where Osama Bin Laden is hiding, are like a maze, a high altitude maze.

The Army Times says, "People who rapidly ascend to high altitudes develop Acute Mountain Sickness: headaches, dizziness, and fatigue. AMS affects the ability of the troops to carry out tasks."

It seems like that's the only footage of Osama Bin Laden, hiking with his friends. Always downhill too. Pretty graceful on those jagged rocks.

The Army also reports having transportation problems in those same mountains. The rough terrain makes it difficult to deliver food and weapons.

Thank God. The doctor says I do not have an STD.

Osama Bin Laden is now raising his AK-47 in the air.

Subject Interview #00136

So our Chief called the division into the conference room. He said some new spots opened up to go kill terrorists and they needed volunteers. Since things were just starting, and not a lot of people had been killed yet, and since our division wasn't really combat folks, because all we did was play around on computers, Chief said we could volunteer and do something really important. Then he said, 'Volunteering won't be an option six months from now, so you might as well go on your own terms.' And guess what, two people raised their hands. They had wanted to kill terrorists anyway. One chick in the front raised her hand and she said, 'Finally, this is the reason I joined.'

So I'm sitting in the back, trying to shrink myself. I do not want to go kill terrorists. This interview is anonymous, right?

Yep. No one will ever know it was you who said this.

Good, because I would never say this aloud but, I do not want to die like everyone else. Anyway, two more people raised their hands. And Chief raised his chin and looked in the back at me, 'What about you.' 'No thank you,' I said, 'not at this moment.' 'It will be good for your career,' he said. 'I plan on getting out soon,' I said.

In the front someone else's hand shot up, 'I'll go, Chief!' The guy walked out and cut his eyes at me and mouthed, 'Fucking pussy.' Chief turned back to me, 'It will be great for your career.' And I'm thinking, why isn't Chief volunteering? Why isn't anyone else raising their fucking hands?

I only enlisted to get the G.I. Bill.
Almost half of my unit was killed.
Most of them enlisted to get the G.I. Bill too.
Next week I have to go on my first deployment.
I can pass away my G.I. Bill to my wife.

Brief History of Navy Slogans

After the draft ended in 1972, the military needed to recruit an "all-volunteer force." The Navy hired professional advertising agencies to design marketing campaigns. The advertising agencies researched target markets and developed plans to sell the Navy.

Be Someone Special (1973 - 1975)

Grey Advertising. 432 offices in 96 countries

About: "Grey's innovative approach to PR is our unparalleled secret weapon. One of the only marketing communications organizations with a full-service public relations team embedded directly within the agency, PR plays a vital role in our collective drive to create Famously Effective work."

Other corporate clients currently include: Botox, Cialis, CoverGirl, Ketel One Vodka, Pfizer, Febreeze, Olive Garden, National Football League, Gillette.

Navy. It's Not Just A Job, It's An Adventure (1976 - 1986)
Live The Adventure (1986 - 1988)

Bates Advertising. 14 offices in 12 countries

About: "Big Ideas for ambitious brands"

Other corporate clients currently include: Johnnie Walker, Every Mother Counts, Lexus, Samsung, PBS, The Wall Street Journal.

You Are Tomorrow; You Are The Navy (1988 – 1990)
You and the Navy: Full Speed Ahead (1990 – 1996)
Let The Journey Begin (1996 - 2000)

BBDO Worldwide. 289 offices in 81 countries, the second largest global advertising agency network. Famous for Burger King's jingle "Have it your way."

About: "At BBDO, we tell stories, both bite-size and long-form. These stories move consumers emotionally and change the way they think, feel or act towards a brand. We then distribute these stories across all relevant channels and screens."

Other corporate clients currently include: Johnson & Johnson, SC Johnson, Campbell's, Starbucks, Mercedes-Benz, Visa, Wells Fargo, Lowe's.

Navy, Accelerate Your Life (2001 - 2009)
America's Navy – A Global Force for Good (2009 - ?)

Lowe Campbell-Ewald: 90 agencies across 65 countries. Famous for Chevrolet's "Like a Rock" campaign.

About: "And who we are is a collective of thinkers, makers, dreamers and doers who come together to create meaningful connections between people and brands."

Other corporate clients currently include: Country Crock, Cadillac, Detroit Lions, Motor City Casino-Hotel, Drug Enforcement Agency, Pasolivo Extra Virgin Olive Oil, United States Mint, Snuggle.

Brief History of Recruiting Posters for Target Markets

TO MAKE MEN FREE

*"..you will share the gratitude of
a nation when victory is ours"*

ENLIST IN THE WAVES TODAY

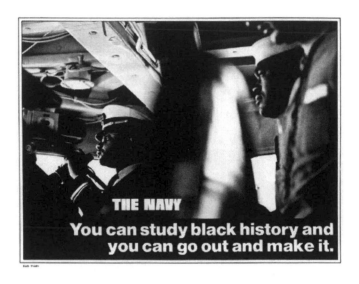

Participation

You take a small boat to the
sub in the middle of the ocean
walk across this shaky bridge
only a foot wide then you form
a chain of people and start
passing bags down the hatch
and passing boxes of food that
say NOT FIT FOR PRISON
USE then you squeeze in your
shoulders bring your hands in
front of your chest put your
feet close together and climb
down this ladder into a tube,
don't forget to duck climb
down about 20 ft and stand in
the galley until someone tells
you where to go everyone else
creeps down the ladder and
piles up next to you someone
squeezes by you and gets pissed
because you're in the way Yes I
chose to be in your way asshole
then a master submarine guy
seats you and tells you all the
things that will kill you if you
don't follow all of these rules
that you don't understand and
everything is

I mean, there's really not much to say, the Navy is great, shipmate. We get paid every two weeks, there's excellent camaraderie, we're keeping the world safe. Pretty simple if you ask me.

Subject Interview #00853

Many did tell amongst themselves, but they were not allowed to ask me. I could not ask for help from others, because I was not allowed to tell. Don't ask. Don't tell. People were already coming to me for makeup advice, food advice, help with sewing or any other bullshit that gay men inherently knew. One time a friend insisted I cut her hair. I told her I didn't know how. She handed me the scissors anyway. I was ignorantly sure that when the scissors touched my hand, some predefined reflex would kick in and I would "go to werk" on her hair. That didn't happen. Instead, I cut a big chunk of her hair out. She didn't speak to me for a week.

I had already heard of one guy being kicked out. We saw each other sometimes but were terrified to speak to each other for fear that we would be each other's undoing. I remember seeing him before he left, looking utterly scared. I didn't want to become him. I tried to express myself through music, science, cooking, work, and academia. I now know it was my desperation to compensate for the immense pressure put on me by the Air Force to keep my mouth shut and not be a liability. Some days were tough, but I kept on. When I went home to Texas, I had a "fuck it" attitude. I went to some gay bars and clubs. After I drank enough, the fear of being snatched by OSI [Office of Special Investigations] or another undercover operative subsided, and I would have a few nights of fun.

Near the end was when I saw "the light." I was already a figure skater and chorister. My apartment was lined up, and I was due to start school. Months before my separation, I sought advice from my seniors and mentors. They all confirmed I was making a terrible mistake. I was warned about the "other side." "You'll be back," one Navy Chief told me.

"You are a very different kind of person ... it is probably for the best," another Air Force Senior told me. I got mostly wishes of good luck surviving than I did wishes of thriving. They all knew I was going to school, singing, skating, but it didn't matter. I bid farewell and parted ways with "America's greatest institution of expeditionary air power" with the idea of it being a great stepping-stone from which I learned a lot.

I sometimes came back for military functions to play music. Having separated in October, I came to the Squadron Christmas party that year. I dyed some of my spiked hair pink and wore a green sweater with a bright pink tie. I was out and proud. Many came up to me in awe asking about life on the other side. I still keep in touch with some of the more progressive people I served with. They too are artistic and ambitious individuals whose views were a bit different for the military, and they too now thrive on "the other side."

Documents

Uniform Code of Military Justice (UCMJ)

ARTICLE 125. SODOMY

(a) Any person subject to this chapter who engages in unnatural carnal copulation with another person of the same or opposite sex or with an animal is guilty of sodomy. Penetration, however slight, is sufficient to complete the offense.

(b) Any person found guilty of sodomy shall be punished as court-martial may direct.

THE NEXT DAY, IN THE COMMANDER'S OFFICE...

SIR, PFC HOWARD REPORTING AS ORDERED.

PFC HOWARD, I'VE RECEIVED A REPORT THAT YOU WERE SEEN ENGAGING IN A HOMOSEXUAL ACT. I CONSIDER THIS INFORMATION TO BE CREDIBLE. I'LL BE CONDUCTING AN INQUIRY AND WOULD LIKE TO ASK YOU SOME QUESTIONS. BUT FIRST I MUST INFORM YOU OF YOUR RIGHTS UNDER ARTICLE 31...

DO YOU UNDERSTAND YOUR RIGHTS AS I EXPLAINED THEM?

YES, SIR, I DO. BUT I DON'T UNDERSTAND WHAT THIS IS ABOUT.

AS I SAID, I RECEIVED A REPORT THAT YOU AND ANOTHER MALE WERE SEEN ENGAGING IN A HOMOSEXUAL ACT IN THE BARRACKS YESTERDAY.

SIR, I WOULD LIKE TO TALK TO A DEFENSE COUNSEL BEFORE MAKING ANY FURTHER STATEMENT.

FINE, PFC HOWARD, I UNDERSTAND. THE 1SG WILL ASSIST YOU TO GET AN APPOINTMENT WITH AN ATTORNEY. BY THE WAY, IF YOU NEED TO TALK WITH SOMEONE ELSE, THE ONLY OTHER PERSON YOU CAN TALK TO IN CONFIDENCE IS THE CHAPLAIN. LET THE 1SG KNOW IF YOU WANT AN APPOINTMENT WITH HIM, TOO.

Nobody else knew, except the other gay dudes of course. And a few of my girl roommates. Hey, do you remember ▮▮▮▮▮ ?

Yeah, that dude was pretty cool.

Yeah, he was. He cracked the door to my gay closet and I came running out with heels on.

Damn. Do you think anyone else found out, I mean, I only knew cuz you told me back in the day. You remember, back when that one girl, I forget her name, was following you around, and I told you that you should just let her suck your dick. And you were like, I don't like girls. I still feel bad about that.

No worries, man. But that was a fucked up thing to say about her.

I know.

But yeah, I think some people had an idea, or maybe a few actually knew, who knows? But luckily I was part of a pretty cool division and people were really nice. I've always appreciated that. But yeah, other than you telling me to let that girl suck my dick, the only other time I've really felt pressure about my sexuality was early on, when I was in Thailand.

We had a hotel room and a bunch of guys off the ship had brought some girls. I was drinking with everyone else, trying to fit in, and actually having a little fun. Everyone was taking turns with the girls, but I wasn't because, you know … plus I was a virgin. But a couple of the guys kept, you know, [Subject makes urging motions with his hands] telling me to 'go get some.' I tried to play it off like I was shy, because

I was back then, well I still am a little, but they wouldn't leave me alone. So I kept drinking, building up my courage I guess. And I took one of the girls to the corner of the room. All could think about was how I was betraying myself, losing my virginity to a girl. I didn't know what I was doing, but it felt good, which made me feel even worse.

Anyway, I had to get the hell out of there, but I wanted to keep up appearances, so I took the girl to my own room. Of course I drank too much and ended up passing out. And she passed out next to me. So to make a long story short, in the morning I found out she was actually a dude.

Participation

We fly from Hawaii to Japan in order to meet the submarine. Once we get on base to check in, our Officer in Charge receives a message from the Fleet Commander that says 'Due to inclement weather, the submarine will not be able to pull into port for at least one more week.' He turns and says, Well, we don't have shit to do. But check in with me at least once a day. I have to physically see you, so let's say, starting tomorrow, muster with me in our hotel lobby every afternoon at 1500.

We check into the Yokosuka Prince Hotel. What! I've never seen people smoking cigarettes while checking into a hotel! I light up too. The ash hanging from my lip falls on my receipt. Our Chief organizes a team lunch at Hard Rock Café. They're all excited. But this is my first time outside the states. I am not eating at Hard Rock Café.

No one wants to go with me anywhere else. And we're not supposed to go anywhere without at least one more person. Guess I'm going to Hard Rock. I sit for a few minutes, then tell them I have jetlag and I'm going back to the hotel. I walk across the street to the train station.

At the train station I find a color-coded railway map. Red, blue, yellow, green, black lines intersect and run parallel and figure eight and split and bunch and peak and valley. Where to go? I close my eyes and circle my finger around the map. Wherever my finger lands. Between Otsuki and Saruhashi. Otsuki.

There are too many lights and buttons on the ticket machine. Spaceship cockpit. I walk to the ticket booth window and point to Otsuki on my map and a man gives me a ticket.

The train pulls away from Yokosuka, blue line on the map, white dots denote cities, I Pac-Man city names: Taura, Higashi-Zushi, Zushi, Yokodai, Negishi, Yamate. Transfer to green line in Yokohama. Continuing past the big Ferris wheel. Grey skyscrapers blur into bright green rice fields spotted with those old houses I've always seen in ninja movies. I wish ninjas were fighting on this train. Fuzzy green and black mountains. I'm hungry. Just a snack.

Off at Nakayama. At one of the stalls I buy a dark purple pickled radish the size of a flashlight. A lot of people are in line at another stall. Must be good. I follow. In line I see people walking from the front with paper cones filled with, crickets? An old lady tosses a few in her mouth. A young man tosses some in his. At the front and a lady is scooping crickets into oil and lightly frying them. I pay for my paper cone and toss a few into my mouth. Alternate: crickets, radish, crickets, radish. I buy a pint of beer from a vending machine.

Another hour and a half and the train pockets into a forest valley. Otsuki. I walk through a park, tree-lined path. Pink and white petals float from the grey sky. At the end of the park I walk into a wooden restaurant and sit at the bar. A woman places a rolled, warm moist towel in front of me. I want to order, but don't know how to ask. The chef starts pressing rice and placing fish on the rice and nodding when he hands it to me. I eat. I never order but the orange red white fish keeps coming. Tiny red balls piled in a crispy seaweed tub. The balls pop between my teeth and salty fish juice squirts. I point to a bottle of, sake? Gulp that shit between bites of fish. I get my bill, do the quick exchange rate, not over my $120 per diem, probably. Fuck it, pull out my government credit card. Stagger back through the dark park to the train station.

35

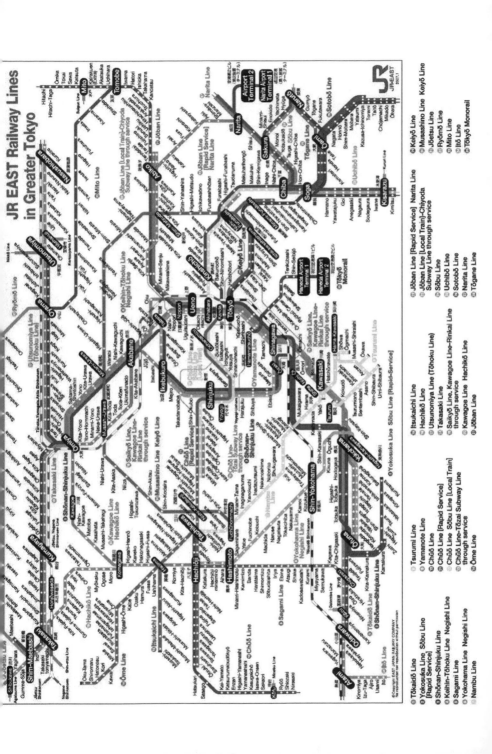

JR EAST Railway Lines in Greater Tokyo

Fuck that map. I know where I'm going, goddammit: Green line southeast to Yokohama, blue line south to Yokosuka. I doze off.

The train jerks me awake. Slowing. Out the window reads Shinjuku. My watch reads 2300. I pull out the map. I got on the wrong line. Almost to Tokyo. Oh well. I don't get off the train until I'm in the heart of Tokyo, whatever that is. I can't recognize any of the shit I've seen on TV.

I turn one corner, another, corner, another. Clubs everywhere. Stinky African men in black and burgundy suits urge me to come to their clubs. Tall Russian prostitutes with thick accents say they want to suck my big black dick. I try to walk into one club but three Japanese men in black suits with slicked back hair cross their arms in an X and say, Japanese only, Japanese only. I say I'm half Japanese. They keep making an X. I scoot to the next club.

Strobe lights, bass, glow sticks swirling, pulsing rainbows, synthesizers. I push my way to the bar. Order a double Bombay Sapphire on the rocks. A blond girl next to me applauds my choice. She yells, How are you doing. I yell, Good. Where are you from, she says. Hawaii, I say, what about you. Canada. She pulls me on the dance floor and I pretend to know how to dance to this music. We go back to the bar. She yells that I need a real drink and orders two American Girls: tall shot glass, red liquor on the bottom, clear in the middle, blue on top. I wonder why it doesn't mix before I pour it down my throat. My eyes water and snot pours out my nose, I can't close my mouth and drool drips to the floor. She's doing the same. We go back to the dance floor. I've resigned to doing jumping jacks while shaking my head yes. She's doing a rain dance. Back to the bar. American Girl. Dance. Bar.

We stumble outside to smoke. She tells me she's teaching English in, somewhere, but comes to Tokyo to party. I tell her I'm on government business, official government business, in Yokosuka. She says, Oh, you're in the military, Navy? Yeah, I'm in a hotel down there, wanna go back with me? She busts out laughing, It's one in the morning, the trains have stopped running. You're stuck here for the night. We can get a hotel here. Sounds gooood, I say. Let's eat first, she says. I follow her down the street and around a corner to a curry house. It's the next day, new $120 per diem. I pay for both our meals. We stagger around the corner, I pay for the hotel with the good ol' government credit card. I wish she was Japanese. This is like eating at Hard Rock. In the room we strip each other's clothes, I hold in my farts from all of that curry.

When I awake she is gone. My watch reads 1237. Good, I can make it back to muster at 1500. Shit, I didn't use a condom. I jump in the shower and wash the white crust off my pubic hair.

I find my way back to the train station. Hop on. On the map there is a big loop around Tokyo, and I need to transfer at Shinagawa. I fall asleep, but when I awake I've missed the transfer, which means I have to ride the train around the loop. I keep falling asleep, missing my transfer, stuck on the loop three times.

I finally make it to Yokosuka. I stroll in the hotel at 1548. My Chief is waiting in the lobby. If you hadn't showed up before 1600 I would've reported you missing, he says. Where were you? Um…I went to Tokyo this morning and it took longer—I don't wanna hear it, he says. You could've been kidnapped by a terrorist and tortured for all I know. Go to your room, and stay.

I am not to be alone until we get back to Hawaii. My Chief assigns me two babysitters. Wherever they go, I am supposed to go. Which means that for the rest of the week, I eat at Hard Rock, KFC, and Pizza Hut. At night I have to go with them to what they call *Buy-Me-Drinkie* bars, where they buy girls drinks that are really teas, but cost double what our drinks cost. My sitters brag to the girls about how they have to take care of me. The girls pretend that they think it's cute. When my sitters buy the girls enough drinks the girls give them hand jobs under the table, or the real deal in a back room. Whenever we leave, my sitters say, Yeah, this is what Japan is all about. They piss on the sidewalks and dare one of those little Japanese fuckers to say something. What are they gonna say, one of my sitters says. We bombed the shit out of their country and took all of their women, they're all pussies. Japanese women want real men. Look at these little pussy cars, they say and laugh. They squat, lift, and roll the tiny car on its side.

The submarine finally pulls in. I stand on the balcony in port and wonder why I volunteered for this.

steel walls steel beds steel toilets steel people. steel

here. stuff head in headphones and listen for   twelve hours
just in case   *ksshhk ksshhk*   maximum unambiguous
range for a radar is twice the speed of light times the pulse
repetition frequency. pulse repetition frequency is the
mathematical inverse of pulse repetition period. frequency
harmonics measured from two to forty gigahertz   *ksshh*
keep listening. pretended listen. pretending listening
kssssssshhhhhk   Dinghai, Xiaopingdao, Jiangzhuang,
Tangshan *ksssh* a radar emitting a small pulse duration with
high pulses per second can [possibly] detect a periscope
depending on synthetic aperture antenna over a target region
to provide finer spatial resolution. i wish i could look out
the periscope. nothing's up there but water

shhh

they're following us we're following them.   paper plates
keep sound down. don't cook in pots and pans   pb & j
pb & j   powdered eggs   pb & j   cup o' noodles
instant oatmeal   pb & j   can we go home?
how about now?   now?
when?

Finally we hit port. Humidity. Back streets. Small pagodas. This is your first time here, my babysitter says, you gotta see this shit. Okay, I slur, I didn't know Thailand was so dirty. We walk around corners, through alleys, people sell meat on sticks, drowned snakes and lizards in whisky bottles. We stumble upon a sort of house building.

We duck our heads and walk to the basement where men sit at tables and women sass around collecting money. We sit at a table toward the front of the stage and order more drinks. The deejay announces something. The other men cheer and whistle. A naked woman walks on stage. She dances, circles her nipples with long fingernails. She lies on her back with a wedge pushing her hips upward. Spreads her legs. And shoots a dart out of her vagina, pops a balloon on the other side of the stage.

Everyone cheers. Mouth open. No tricks, my sitter says, That's the real goddamn deal. The deejay places a stack of quarters on the stage. She does a split over the quarters. When she stands the quarters are gone. She walks to our table and motions me to pull her arm down like a slot machine. Out comes the quarters one by one. She leaves the stage. I wonder where she lives. How does she know this stuff. We fly back to Hawaii first-class.

Brief History

"The importance of Thailand in the global sex industry is generally traced back to the late 1960s with the use of Thailand as a place for "rest and recreation" for American G.I.s in Vietnam. The recommendation by the World Bank in the 1970s that Thailand develop "mass tourism" as a means to pay off its debts, encouraged what became the peace-time institutionalization of the sex industry in Thailand."

—Joan Nagel in *Race, Ethnicity, and Sexuality* (2003), quoting Phil Williams, *Trafficking in Women and Children: A Market Perspective* (1999)

Prayer for Peace

Lord, make me an instrument of
 Your peace.
Where there is hatred, let me sow
 love.
Where there is injury, pardon,
Where there is doubt, faith,
Where there is despair, hope,
Where there is darkness, light,
 and where there is sadness, joy.
O Divine Master, grant that I may
 not so much seek to be consoled,
 as to console;
To be understood, as to understand;
To be loved, as to love;
For it is in giving that we receive
It is in pardoning that we are
 pardoned;
And it is in dying that we are
 born to eternal life.

St. Francis of Assisi

800-241

MADE IN ITALY

ubject Interview #32001

ircumstance, be in or on this.

ought I told you it would be

n this, it can be linked back
n't want that.

n the acknowledgements.

here.

being a "Military Spouse"
absolutely fucking sucks. No glitter and twilight here. It
just sucks. The housing and healthcare aren't truly free, and
unbroken hours at home. And a lot of these other spouses
are nosey and quick to talk shit. Welcome to the great
world of being a Military Spouse!

Yes, I know I chose this life. But it's a life I hate. A life
that is just brutally mundane. My husband is gone seventy-
five percent of the time, ranging from a few days to over
half a year at times. Hell, I didn't even get to celebrate the
"honeymoon" period for the first three years of my marriage.
That's how much he was gone. Then you add the lack of
friends in military housing. Then you add children, who you
are caring for alone. ALONE.

The spousal support groups available are sporadic at best. Your
best bet is to reach outside to the civilian sector. Because the

reality is, the military support groups are just like a group of grown high-school women. If you love gossip and affairs, then you'll fit right in. And since the support groups are connected to the military, there is absolutely no privacy. What you say can be reported to your spouse's command, and your spouse could get in trouble. They aren't all bad honestly, but for the most part, they are just like that. I've experienced both sides, civilian and military support groups.

And oh, you're sick? Welcome to the best healthcare known to man: TRICARE. Now don't get me wrong. They do come through when it comes to "serious" illnesses. But if it's not "serious," TRICARE is a pain in the ass. Referrals take weeks to complete. Sometimes, you don't even live close to a military hospital and risk having a hefty ER bill if they decide it wasn't "serious" enough for them to cover. And God forbid you choose to stay with standard coverage, as we have chosen due to our child's needs. They only cover about fifty percent of your doctor's visit, and the rest, well that's up to you to figure out. TRICARE doesn't even cover marriage counseling.

The moving every few years, the fluttering changes of friends, the world ending every deployment, the headaches. That is what it's like as a spouse. Long hours and isolation. Fights due to loneliness. Nosey neighbors. Walking, talking mannequins. Affairs. Insecurity. Bitterness. No communication.

As I've said, these are all firsthand experiences, but I'm not alone in feeling this way. And that's why I think military members and spouses are all high horse patriotic and shit. I mean, you gotta make yourself believe you're supporting a greater good because of how horrible this life is.

Subject Interview #00083

I loved her. I think. I'm not so sure about that word. I mean, I love love, in theory. Theory is beautiful, but love in the real world is something else. I'm at work every day with people who love their country, love god, love ice cream, love getting fucked up. I think it's wonderful that one can use the same word of affection for country and ice cream. But the thing with ice cream is, when your tastes change, you can say you love this new flavor of ice cream better than you loved that old disgusting butterscotch. You can't do that with a country.

Anyway, I loved most things about her, especially her red hair. We'd joke that our kids would have grey skin and burgundy hair. Only one of them did. The other two had tan skin and brown hair like regular mixed children. The kids are fine now, I think.

Anyway, I really loved most things about her, especially her voice. That's why I pretended not to listen so she wouldn't stop talking. She'd say, Can you please get out the Navy. Over and over. Please get out, she'd say, being with the kids by myself all the time is killing me. I liked the sound of her voice so much that's the only thing I focused on, just the sound.

Anyway, she'd try to cope, write it all out: journals, pros and cons, and optimistic analogies. I had just returned from back-to-back twelve-month deployments (I came home for a week between the two.) She was sitting on the floor in our bedroom upstairs with that lovely red hair all wild like it was reaching out to me. I walked in and she said, I've been working on these analogies for two years, making progress. Maybe you can help. I said, Great, I'll be right back, I gotta go get a drink first, then call my Chief, something hilarious happened.

I came back and she was gone. Just gone. The only things left were a powdery burgundy residue in the shape of her butt and crossed legs where she'd been sitting, and her notebook, with the optimistic analogies:

My husband being in the Navy is like my husband being in the Navy. Deployments are to deployments as deployments are to deployments. Love is to country as love is to ice cream.

Participation

Our command gives us the opportunity to volunteer at a local elementary school, reading stories to the children, and helping the teachers with whatever they need, like setting out Elmer's and picking up crayons and making sure the kids don't cut themselves with scissors or construction paper.

The kids have big smiles, big eyes, and big mouths. One girl says, "I'm Filipina, Japanese, Portuguese, and Thai." A boy says, "My family is from Samoa and Korea and China *and* Taiwan." The teacher tells me that's just how it is in Hawaii, most people are so mixed up here, and that's what makes it beautiful.

I tell the kids I'm from West Virginia. "West Virginia?" they say, "What's that?" I tell them it's a state on the mainland, kinda close to New York. They ask me what I am. "Black," I say, "just black." The Filipina-Japanese-Portuguese-Thai girl says, "So you're just one thing? No way!" The other kids crack up and start singing, "Just one thiiing, just one thiiing." Another girl shouts above the chanting, "So what, I'm just one thing too, I'm Korean."

The teacher quiets them and gives me a book to read called *There Was an Old Auntie*. I say it like this: *awn-tee*. But the kids tell me it's: *an-tee*. They tell me I talk funny. They talk funny too. I finally finish the book after multiple interruptions because of my multiple mispronunciations.

The teacher tells the kids to say thank you to me, and to the Navy for sending volunteers. One boy says he sees all the ships at Pearl Harbor and asks me do I get to shoot the big guns on the big ships. "No," I say, "but hanging out with y'all today is my favorite thing I've ever done in the Navy."

"But you didn't shoot any guns today," he says. One girl says her dad was in the Navy but he went to the mainland with another wife and never ever came back since I was a baby.

Another boy says his uncle is in the Navy and has the coolest stories in the whole wide world, he even saw a Japanese mermaid, and she was sooo beautiful. "I wanna be a mermaid," the Korean girl says. "I am a mermaid," says the Filipina-Japanese-Portuguese-Thai girl. Some other kids tell her she is a liar and her pants are on fire.

The teacher says she thought the kids loved me, apologized for their teasing, and that she'd love for me to come back. "I'm sure the Navy wouldn't mind," I say, "They encourage us to get out in the community and help out."

Subject Interview #00872

Alright, this is how I got over on the Navy. I remember, after my first enlistment, I was at my five-year mark and I wanted to re-enlist, only so I could get a re-enlistment bonus. But, they told me in order to reenlist and get the forty grand, I had to go to C School, but they didn't have the money to send me to C School. So I was like, you know what, I'll extend for a year, and take the same classes on base, and that way, I can get the same C School credentials and get the forty grand, without them having to pay to send me to C School. That make sense?

Yeah.

Alright. So, I extended for one year and took two classes: Basic Signals Analysis and Intermediate Signals Analysis, but the next class wasn't available until a year later, so I extended for *another* year. That made it seven years. And the last year I took Advanced Signals Analysis. And at the end of the class they were like, Okay, you now have the full qualifications of what you would've gotten in C School. So when I went to talk to the C.O. she was like, Okay, um, we gonna get you to reenlist for another six years and get forty thousand dollars. And I was like, you know what, I'm not gonna re-enlist. Imma just get out and use those same credentials to get a civilian job. And the C.O looked me dead in my face and said, If I knew that I would've never let you taken those classes. And I got a good-ass job too, eighty grand a year, nigga. Fuck that punk-ass forty grand.

Participation

Our command says the Hawaii Foodbank needs volunteers for the quarterly food drive. About 30 of us sign up. On Saturday we're supposed to be at the Foodbank waaaay on the other side of the island at 0700. But since the Navy tells us that if you show up on time, you're late, which means that 0645 is actually on time for us. And to make sure we are nowhere near late *or* on time, we all show up at 0630, ready. To "help move, sort, shrink-wrap & weigh very large quantities of canned and dry food donations." The volunteer coordinator pulls in, happy with the amount of us who showed up, and puts us to work right away.

Only three of my shipmates say they are hung over, but they're still lifting and shrink-wrapping like crazy. Two of my shipmates say they were at the strip club until 0400. "We still made it, though," they say, "but if we would've got lucky, you all would've been shrink-wrapping by your damn selves."

Throughout the day, people drive up and donate food, mostly Spam and rice. A few cans of beans, shells and cheese, some Top Ramen. We sort the food into specified bins on wooden pallets, weigh the bins, and use the pallet jack to push or pull the food into the warehouse. During lunch, the volunteer coordinator hands us pamphlets about the importance of the food drive.

Homes in Hawaii:

- 62% report choosing between paying for food and paying for utilities.
- 62% report making choices between paying for food and paying for transportation.
- 56% report choosing between paying for food and paying for medicine/medical care.

At the end of the day, 4:30 pm, all pallets of food are weighed and added, and we have collected 3,819 pounds of food and we are not sure if that is a lot, it seems like a lot, but I guess we won't find out until next year if the percentages decrease for the amount of people who choose between paying for food or utilities or education or housing.

Back at our command on Monday, I overhear one of my shipmates who was at the strip club arguing with our Chiefs about his brag sheet. A brag sheet is what we must write before we receive our evaluations, which factor in heavily for advancement. On the brag sheet, we are supposed to list what we did over the last quarter, like how many days we've been out to sea, if we've taken any college courses, any awards, how much training we've completed, and how many hours we've spent volunteering.

Our Chiefs are pleading with/threatening him to put his volunteer hours on his brag sheet. They tell him they know he has volunteered at the elementary school, at the food drive, at carwashes, at Habitat for Humanity, at homeless shelters; and these things reflect well on himself as well as the Navy, and if he doesn't include these things, his evaluation will be worth a shiny quarter in a pile of dog shit.

"I don't volunteer for you fuckers, or the fucking Navy, I volunteer for myself, because *I* want to." The Chiefs tell him to lower your voice, son, you're getting out of line. "You're out of line, trying to tell me what to do with my own volunteer time." They correct him, and tell him that he *has*, in fact, volunteered during working hours, and besides, *you* don't have any time, because *your* time is the Navy's time; you're in the Navy 24-7, son.

Later, our Chiefs call us to a mandatory meeting, "We just want to reiterate the importance of your brag sheets. No one knows more about what you did, than you. We want to give you the credit you deserve, that's why it would behoove you, to include everything, you have done, on your brag sheets."

I put all my volunteer hours on my brag sheet. The guy still refused to, plus he got written up for insubordination, and his evaluation noted that he is an average sailor who needs to take on more responsibility and learn how to foster respect up and down the chain-of-command.

A Break from the Navy: Home on Leave

No thinking about the Navy for three weeks. I can already taste my aunt's fried fish and my cousin's Purple Haze.

At my folks' house I hug my sisters and my mom and dad. Glad you made it home, my mom says, Thanks for protecting us. My sister rolls her eyes and points to a sticker on the refrigerator: Proud Navy Mom

I'm outside smoking cigarettes with my dad and his friends. One of his friends says, You still in that Army? No, I'm in the Navy. He says, It's good you joined the Army. I tried to get my boy to sign-up but that sorry-ass nigga don't wanna do shit but smoke dope and lay around with these no-good hoes. You should get him to join, he says, Tell him how much of that Chinese pussy you gettin in Japan.

Ain't you a spy? No, I say. Oh, he says, you'd have to kill us if you told us, huh? I stub out my cigarette and throw it into the garbage can because my mom just swept the sidewalk. My dad's friend says, Uncle Sam got that boy trained good—he don't leave no tracks behind.

My dad says, Yall ain't find that one muthafucka yet? No, I say. And yall ain't gon find him—he probably still in New York. I ain't believin shit that lyin-ass news say, they know he aint in no Zackitstan, Crackistan, he ain't in nown one of them goddamn *Stans*.

My mom sends me to the Post Office. In the Post Office there is a Wall of Heroes with a photo of everyone from our town who is currently in, or has been in the Armed Forces. Even if they were kicked out for drugs or attempted suicides or check fraud or going AWOL. There is photo of me from boot camp, the cheesy one with the soft grey background. I have on that silly white hat and a serious look on my child face. I snatch my picture down, crumple it, and toss it in the trash.

Miss Alice walks in, How you been, baby? The Army treating you good? Yes ma'am. Reach up there and get my mail. I keep telling these dern folks to move my box down. They late again with my Social Security. Now I done seen a picture of you up on that wall. Where is it now? Imma have to get ya mama to talk to these folks, see if they can get a picture of you up there. Alright now, you be good in that Army, and don't get kicked out like some of these snot-nosed hoodlums, they ain't worth a dern, takin drugs and all kinds of devilish mess.

I walk outside and see Earl Jr. I act like I'm in a hurry but he grabs my shoulders and hugs me. I see ol' Uncle Sam got you doing them push-ups, he says, makin a man outta you. He punches me in the chest. Goddamn, almost broke my fist. I say, I gotta get ba— Now, now, hold on a minute, he says. Now ya mama done told me you was on them submarines. Yeah, I say. I already knowed it! See, I was up there fishin, up there at Brewster Lake, and a submarine just *bust* up out the water, scared all damn my fish off. And that's when I saw you, right there on that submarine.

****

That night I go to my friend's house. He invites a few more people over. I always say the same thing, What yall been up to? They always say the same thing, Nothin, you know ain't shit to do round here. I shoulda joined the service too, but I ain't want nobody yelling in my face and telling me what to do.

I give my friend forty for the weed and open the bottle of Hennessey I bought. Our homegirl says, Mr. Military Man, makin that *good* money. Terrell says, That *easy* money. That nigga ain't out here grindin in the streets like us.

My friend asks me about Japan. I tell him I love it, especially the food. Terrell says, I betcha that General Tso's be good as hell over there. That's Chinese food, I say. Uppity muthafucka, Terrell says. Niggas move away and think they better than everybody. Anybody can join a fuckin Navy. Shut the fuck up, my friend says, If it was so easy why you ain't do it. Cuz nigga, Terrell says, I ain't joinin some white man's military, ain't nothing but poor folks dyin for rich white folks.

My friend passes me the joint. I hit it and pass it back. For real though, my friend says, How you like that shit? It's alright, I say. You don't like shootin muthafuckas and blowing shit up? Nope. You crazy, he says, I'd be blowing all types of shit up. On some real shit though, he says, It's a good thing you got from around here, this place is a fuckin trap, ain't nobody goin nowhere. Milk that shit for all it's worth, man, and get the fuck out and do you.

****

The next day my cousin comes home because he heard I was home. He joined the Navy a few months before I did. He pulls up in a new blue Chevy with chrome rims and hops out with his uniform on. Some of our friends walk over and he gives everyone dap and hugs them with his free arm. Some of the kids run over and give my cousin hi-fives. He gives them five dollars each and tells them to go buy some candy, some good candy. His mom comes out smiling and hugs us, Thank the Lord! His dad follows, Look at these Navy men! Out there fightin the good fight! I know yall gonna get them twenty years in. My cousin says, You know it! I say, Maybe. Maybe my ass, my uncle says, You better do them twenty and get that pension.

My cousin takes off his little white hat and sits on his tailgate. Brandon points to my cousin's chest, What's that for? He says, It's a Naval Achievement Medal. I received it for being responsible for the operation and maintenance of missile launching systems and other ordnance equipment. That's some good shit right there, Brandon says, you doin ya thang, homie.

My cousin says, Your mom told me to come down to the school. My mom is a cook at the elementary school. One cook's son joined the Marines. My last time here, my mom and the other lady bantered about which branch was better. The argument ended once the lady told my mom that all branches are important because they serve God and country.

My cousin also wants to see our old principal. Why? I say. Because he made me realize that leading from the front is not a part-time job—it is what we must do every minute of every day we are called to serve.

We walk into our principal's office. He stands and salutes. And asks me why I'm wearing sweatpants. He says something about leading from the front.

We walk through the halls and stop at each classroom to see my cousin's favorite teachers. They all smile and hug. The kids ooh and aah.

In the kitchen my mom and her co-workers make my cousin spin with his uniform on. They tell me to go get mine. I tell them I didn't bring it.

I tell my friend that his dad wanted me to convince him to join the Army. Fuck him, he says, and fuck the military.

My sister told me she thought about signing up. I told her that men rape women too much in the military. She said, That's not special, it's the same thing happening out here.

I asked a man at the strip club for a military discount. He said, Anything for a hero.

I asked a woman at the movie theater for a military discount. She said, What the fuck for?

I think about not going back. Where else could I go? It doesn't matter. I can't go anywhere.

Subject Interview XXXXX

Do you really think I'm going to sit here and let you interview me? I saw that story you wrote about you smoking weed. Why would you include something like that? You're making the Navy look bad. All I know is, you'd better be careful. This country you so willingly insult is the reason you have the freedom of speech to write that stupid book of yours.

Subject # 00215

He's better than he used to be, but my brother has never been a very adventurous eater. When he was a kid, only wanted to eat meat, potatoes, and chocolate cake. This is maybe disgusting, but the way we used to split cans of Chunky soup as kids was for him to pick all the vegetables except for potatoes out of his bowl and put them in mine, and then I'd scoop all of my meat into his.

When he was in the army, he said, "The food tastes like school cafeteria food, but I don't mind it." It was different when he was "down range." The food was too bland, even for him. When I sent care packages, they'd be full of Doritos and cigarettes.

"Does your sister think you're in jail?" someone asked.

They had Afghan food night at the commissary, and he figured he'd try it. He couldn't leave the army base, and it was the only foreign country he'd ever been to, so it was the only way he'd really experience the culture. It was awful, he said, just as bland as everything else, just as gray and miserable.

When he was working overnights during Ramadan, the locals that worked on base would happen to break their fast at the same time he was having dinner. Someone had told him the food was better this time around, or he was feeling brave, or maybe the line was just the shortest, so he decided to give it another shot. It was glorious, he said. So delicious and perfectly seasoned and unlike anything he'd ever had before in his life.

My brother is one of those guys that people just like right away, the kind of guy who can make a person laugh while he's making fun of them, but he's shy about his military service. He didn't relate to a lot of the guys he was in the army with, and now that he's out, he doesn't want people to think he's like that, you know, hateful or stupid or bigoted.

When he got out, he started working at the same coffee shop where he'd worked before he left for basic training. And almost every day for lunch, he'd go to what he decided was the best halal cart. He'd always be the first in line, just shooting the shit with the guy who worked the cart, while the oil heated so he could fry up the first falafel of the day.

Tariq was just as friendly as he was, so my brother learned a lot about his life pretty quickly. He'd come here from Afghanistan, via Pakistan because he had to flee the Taliban, and was now working in this cart, but didn't own it. My brother didn't want to risk losing his favorite lunch by telling Tariq that he'd been to Afghanistan, as an "invader", so he mostly listened, until one day, when Tariq was gossiping about someone who wasn't as generous, not as hospitable as his people, and my brother asked, "Is that because he's not a Pashtun, like you?"

"You know my people?" Tariq lit up. It was probably the first time my brother told someone who wasn't offering him a military discount that he'd been in the army.

There are few Afghani restaurants here in Philly. Two of them are on the same block and have been open for years and years. My brother had been wanting to go to one, because he likes the food so much, but feels terrible about how he came to like the food, so it took probably a year after he left the military before he went. He took a date, and told me that he was crying while stuffing lamb and rice into his mouth.

He went back, this time with me and a few friends. It was a weeknight, and we were the only people in the place. It was lived in, a little crowded with decor, hadn't been updated since they opened in the early 90's. The food was wonderful, familiar and mysterious all at once. The owner doted on us, and I asked my brother, who was crying again, if he was going to say something to him about why he liked Afghani food.

"Oh, no. I don't know how he feels about what happened over there. I just want to keep eating here."

Participation

For Veterans' Day we all go to this chain restaurant and get free burgers or steaks or molten lava cakes. The staff thanks each and every one of us as we walk in. They thank us when we sit. They thank us when they bring our meals.

On the televisions, the same news channel shows a montage of soldiers surprising their loved-ones at baseball games, jobs, grocery stores, clarinet recitals, PTA meetings, dentist appointments. The kids and the wives and the husbands are crying and running and jumping on the soldiers and squeezing and squeezing. Country music plays in the background. Our eyes swell with tears.

Why. I wouldn't wanna hug that dude. I don't even wanna hug myself. He might need to be hugged. Of course his family missed him. He could've not returned. He made other people not return. I made people not return.

In the bathroom I vomit my free burger. I walk out. The hostess thanks me for my service. I thank her for her service in order to avoid saying You're Welcome. She looks confused, No, *thank you*. I don't respond. She thanks the guy behind me for his service. No problem, he says, we do it for you.

service (n.)

c.1100, "celebration of public worship," from Old French *servise* "act of homage; servitude; service at table; Mass, church ceremony," from Latin *servitium* "slavery, condition of a slave, servitude," also "slaves collectively," from servus "slave" (***see serve*** (v.)).

serve (v.)

late 12c., "to render habitual obedience to," also "minister, give aid, give help," from Old French *servir* "to do duty toward, show devotion to; set table, serve at table; offer, provide with," from Latin *servire* "be a servant, be in service, be enslaved;" figuratively "be devoted; be governed by; comply with; conform; flatter," originally "be a slave."

Field Notes

I have made a decision. I have made a decision to not say or feel that I serve. I will only say and feel that I work in the military. Work. I am trying to build a linguistic fence around myself. I do not serve. But I am going on deployment next week and we will shoot missiles that will kill people. My fence is breaking down. I work in the military. I serve the military.

Participation

Although I have declined numerous times, it is mandatory that I attend a Career Development Board. Four Chiefs sit around a table and help me develop my career.

So, Petty Officer, what can you do to advance?
I'm not interested in advancing.
Why not?
I'm just not interested.
Well, what are your long-range goals?
To get out the Navy.
Okay. So what are your mid-range goals?
To get out the Navy.
Well then, shipmate, what are your short-range goals?
To get out the Navy.
But you have six years left.

Field Notes

Items of consideration to reach my short-range goals:

- ~~Don't clean my system out the next time I get high~~
- ~~Punch an officer in the face~~
- Get fat and fail three consecutive PT tests
- Study really hard in order to miss every answer on advancement exams
- ~~Get three DUIs~~
- ~~Go AWOL~~
- ~~Disobey direct orders and shit~~
- Kiss another man at work

Damn, I can't do some of those because I'll get a Dishonorable Discharge, and I need to get out on an Honorable or Administrative, cuz I still want my G.I. Bill. Plus it's hard to get a job if they see you had a Dishonorable. You can't even work at the fucking Post Office with a Dishonorable.

Participation

We file into ranks for Quarters, our daily morning meeting. The Chief, and the Leading Petty Officer (LPO), and the Assistant Leading Petty Officer (ALPO), saunter between the rows, inspecting our uniforms. Chief stops at one person, pulls out his I.D card, and rakes it against the person's chin to see if he has shaved.

"Go shave immediately," Chief says. The guy takes one step backwards, spins on his heels, and marches out of formation. We shuffle down to fill his space. Chief continues his inspection.

The LPO follows Chief and whispers to me, "You shitbags are gonna get it today."

The ALPO follows, "Yeah, you shitbags are gonna get it today."

Chief, the LPO, and the ALPO walk in front of the formation. Chief spreads his legs shoulder width and crosses his arms. He nods while staring side to side. The Division Officer walks out and stands next to the Chief. "I've been noticing a lack of morale," the Division Officer says, "and a serious lack of appreciation for the sacrifices made by those who came before you. Anything to add, Chief?"

Chief steps up, "I'd just like to reiterate what the Division Officer said. I too have noticed a lack of morale," Chief scans the formation, "and a *gravely* serious lack of appreciation for the sacrifices made by the brave men and women that have come before you. Anything to add, LPO?"

The LPO says he would like to reiterate.

The ALPO says he would also like to reiterate.

The Division Officer asks Chief what is he going to do about it. Chief smiles with his lips closed. He says, "We're going to a special place, a special place we're gonna go to together as a unit. A *very* special place where you will learn to revitalize and re-energize your appreciation and boost your morale. We are going to The Taxidermy Museum of Military Heroes."

Subject Interview #03962

We lost a lot of good men over there.

Were any bad men lost?

Participation

At The Taxidermy Museum of Military Heroes we saw a bunch of people who received Medals of Honor or Purple Hearts. There was a teenage girl whose parents made her go for the same reason our Chief made us go. She said she'd stolen something from the Base Exchange and her dad said that courageous people were dying for her freedom and she was throwing away that freedom for some silly punk rock boots.

The girl and I were standing next to a VOLUNTEERS WANTED sign and looking at a diorama containing a taxidermied marine who'd been awarded a Purple Heart. "When I was little, my dad told me that my grandfather had gotten a Purple Heart," she told me, "I thought it was some type of medical condition. I imagined my grandfather's heart all swollen and turning purple until he died."

I pointed to the sign and jokingly told her she should volunteer. "I think my dad is gonna make me," she said, "for real."

Subject Interview # 80023

I am extremely proud of what I did for my country. We're the good guys, you know. I put on that uniform every morning and held my chest out and chin up, knowing I was doing some real good in the world. I know my arm won't grow back, but I have absolutely no regrets. [*Subject wipes away a tear.*] If God was willing, I would do it all over again. Yeah, all over again.

Participation

I volunteered to work at the Taxidermy Museum of Military Heroes. It gets me out of work three days a week, plus it looks like I'm taking on extra duties for my bragsheet.

Towering the expansive asphalt parking lot is the mirrored atrium, tapering to apex, giving way to sleek white façades branched into four wings, a cross. On each side of the atrium is a circle of flagpoles. On each flagpole an American flag droops halfway down. A plaque reads: *These flags will forever be flown at half-staff in honor of the heroes who gave their lives for freedom.* Inside the circle of flagpoles is a bronze statue lying with arms out, palms to heaven, helmet cocked. Adjacent bronze rifle. Scattered bronze bullet casings.

I walk inside the atrium. Conditioned air envelops me while stained glass pools rainbows onto marble floors. In the center of the atrium, underneath the apex, and raised on a platform is a soldier, taxidermied. He crouches in shooting position, stuffed white fingers curled around rifle trigger, one eye squints, the other eyeball stares straight ahead.

I am supposed to meet the Lead Taxidermist for orientation. She descends on the escalator behind the soldier. I see you're admiring our work, she says looking over her glasses and placing a loose, grey dreadlock behind her ear. Yes, I say, It looks really life-like. She says, Honey, we are all *life-like.* Huh? I say. I understand what you're saying, she says. But what I'm saying is, we only live in approximation to life, approaching what life *is.* Even dying is attempting to approach life. That's how I perceive taxidermy. A representation of extant *and* extinct humans in that liminal space of approaching life.

Subject Interview #02509

Of course, sugar, I'll answer any questions you want.

How did you come into this line of work?

Well, for twenty years I'd specialized in taxidermy for the other Great Apes: Chimpanzees, Gorillas, Bonobos, Orangutans. So the government contacted me when they dreamed up this little project of preserving Humans, the other Great Ape. They'd seen my work in various museums around the world. Most notably, the Zoologisk Museum at the University of Copenhagen in Denmark, where I taxied a Silverback Gorilla and his entire harem of four females along with two infants. Somehow they'd been poisoned in the Congo, The Democratic Republic. Gotta get the names right since you're publishing this. Anyway, lots of parallels can be drawn between performing taxidermy on the other Great Apes and Humans. Although bipedalism and glabrescence present their own particular sets of challenges, which we can discuss later.

I'm sorry, what does 'glabrescence' mean?

Oh don't be sorry. It's a pesky word anyway. It's the technical term for hairlessness. And do me a favor, please. Make sure you capitalize the names of the animals, they're proper names in my book.

[*Subject gives me a copy of her book*, Flesh of My Flesh: The Liminal Space of Taxidermy.]

Documents

Some things I have Signed:
In terms of Body and Behavior

The military has its own laws, rules,

c. A member may be discharged by reason of parenthood

if it is determined the member,

because of parental responsibilities,

is unable to perform his or her duties satisfactorily or is

unavailable for worldwide assignment or deployment.

d. A member may be separated for violation of laws or regula... ns regarding sexual conduct
of members of the Armed Forces, for example, ...aging or atten...ing to engage in a
homosexual ... or soliciting another to engage ...uch an act; fo... ...ati...hat he or she is a
homosexual ...bisexual, or words to that effec... for marrying ...tte... ...ing to marry an
individual of ... same sex. See reverse.

RESTRICTIONS ON ... SONAL CONDU... ...E ARMED FORCES

WARNING

Failure to disclose any information about
by a $10,000 fine, 5 years in prison or both.

CLEAN SLATE DISCLOSURE FORM

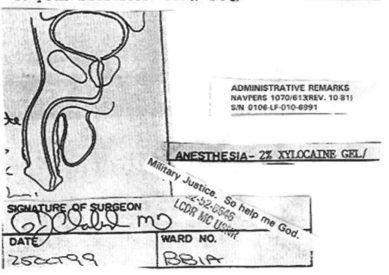

1. EDUCATION: Have you graduated
from High School? Yes(✓) No()
Have you completed any college or
vocational school? Yes() No(✓)
Have you provided transcript copies
to your recruiter? Yes() No(✓)

ADMINISTRATIVE REMARKS
NAVPERS 1070/613(REV. 10-81)
S/N 0106-LF-010-6991

ANESTHESIA- 2% XYLOCAINE GEL/

Military Justice. So help me God.

2-52-6546
LCDR MC USNR

SIGNATURE OF SURGEON

DATE
25OCT99

WARD NO.
BB1A

Suicidal/homicidal: No
Client denied suicidal/homicidal ideation plan or intent.

Reason for Appointment: healthy thinking
Appointment Comments:

I HEREBY VOLUNTEER FOR DUTY IN A SUBMARINE

Hazing is not part of our "time honored traditions"

Alleged Offender's Relationship To Victim: Intrafamilial/Spouse
Type of Maltreatment: Minor physical

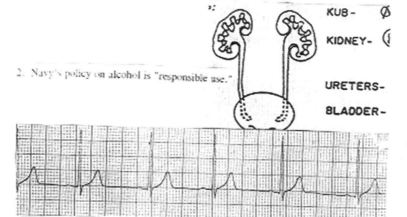

KUB -

KIDNEY -

2. Navy's policy on alcohol is "responsible use."

URETERS-

BLADDER-

OFFENSE: Violation of UCMJ Art.86, Absence without leave
Violation of UCMJ Art. 91, Insubordinate conduct towards a noncommissioned officer
Violation of UCMJ Art 92 Failure to obey order or regulation

PUNISHMENT AWARDED: Reduction to next inferior pay grade

Participation

The Lead Taxidermist unlocks a Staff Only door and we walk down. There are four levels of the basement, she says, each is for a different part of the process. We descend three flights of concrete stairs, lit by emergency-exit-green.

On the third level we walk into a room. Fluorescent lights hum a glow onto white tiled walls, glossy white floors with black flecks, gun-grey cabinets. A 20 x 20 grid of stainless steel tables with sinks at each end, and evenly spaced holes in the top surface. I circle my finger along one of the holes. To collect the drippings, she says.

The Lead Taxidermist zigzags from room to room. *Taxi*, means to arrange, she says, and of course, *derm*, means skin. She walks over to a stainless steel cabinet with a glass door, digital red numbers: Five degrees Celsius. These are ready to be mounted, she says pointing with a pen. Flesh hangs, short-sleeved, rounded at the bottom like shirttails. Droopy black holes where eyes once were.

Right now, this is the only processing center, she says. We will begin shipping taxidermy to the five other museums being built around the country until they are fitted with their own processing centers. Lord knows when, but hopefully soon, we're so backlogged here.

This way, she says. At the end of the room is a large door, digital red again: Zero degrees Celsius. Hanging next to the door is a clipboard, white paper rows and columns filled with text. This is our storage room for the bodies waiting to be taxied.

Inside the room, gush of cold vacuum-sealed air, Stainless steel ceilings revealed by successive motion-detected fluorescents. Stainless steel trays stacked four high, four wide, separated by an aisle. Four more trays, another aisle, and I can't tell how far back they go. Each tray holds a stiff body, face up, covered by a white sheet.

Table	Name	Rank	Branch	Age	Date of Death	Cause of Death	Place of Death	Cremate?
1		Captain	Army	30	9/29	Non-hostile – suicide	Baghdad	Y
2		Lance Corporal	Marines	19	10/14	Hostile Fire - IED attack	Baghdad	Y
3		Corporal	Marines	21	10/14	Hostile Fire – IED attack	Baghdad	Y
4		Specialist	Army	23	10/09	Hostile Fire – small arms fire	Baghdad	N
5		1st Lieutenant	Army	25	9/30	Hostile Fire – helicopter crash	Baghdad	Y
6		Sergeant	Army	28	9/28	Non-Hostile-suicide	Al Amarah	Y
7		Captain	Army	27	9/30	Hostile Fire – rocket attack	Wasit	Y
8		Specialist	Army	22	10/02	Non-Hostile-suicide	Wasit	N
9		Specialist	Army	21	10/05	Non-Hostile-suicide	Wasit	N
10		Specialist	Army N.G.	20	10/05	Hostile Fire – rocket attack	Wasit	Y
11		Private 1st Class	Army	19	10/31	Hostile Fire - grenade	Tikrit	Y
12		Commander	Army	49	9/03	Hostile Fire-suicide car bomb	Manama	Y
13		Corporal	Marines	25	9/01	Hostile Fire-suicide car bomb	Badrah	Y
14		Lance Corporal	Marines	26	9/01	Hostile Fire-suicide car bomb	Diyala	Y
15		Corporal	Army	22	8/29	Non-Hostile-friendly fire	Kandahar	N
16		Staff Sergeant	Army	23	8/29	Non-Hostile-friendly fire	Kandahar	Y
17		Staff Sergeant	Army	24	8/29	Non-Hostile-friendly fire	Kandahar	Y
18		Private 2nd Class	Army	19	8/29	Non-Hostile-friendly fire	Kandahar	Y
19		Specialist	Army	25	8/29	Non-Hostile-friendly fire	Kandahar	Y
20		Major General	Army	55	9/17	Non-Hostile-illness	Kabul	Y
21		Petty Officer 2nd	Navy	23	10/02	Non-Hostile-vehicle accident	Bagram AFB	N
22		Chief Petty Off.	Navy	35	10/02	Non-Hostile-vehicle accident	Bagram AFB	Y
23		Airman 1st Class	Air Force	24	10/05	Hostile Fire-small arms fire	Bagram AFB	Y
24		Tech. Sergeant	Air Force	30	10/06	Hostile Fire-small arms fire	Bagram AFB	Y
25		Gunnery Sgt.	Marines	35	9/23	Hostile Fire-IED attack	Patika	Y
26		Gunnery Sgt.	Marines	34	9/23	Hostile Fire-IED attack	Patika	Y
27		Private	Marines	19	9/17	Non-Hostile-suicide	Baghdad	N
28		Private	Marines	19	9/18	Non-Hostile-suicide	Baghdad	Y
29		Private 1st Class	Army	20	9/19	Non-Hostile-suicide	Kabul	Y

We have to be careful not to let the temperature of this room fall below zero, she says, because ice will form in the body tissue and the skin will lose its wonderful elasticity. Hell, even at this temperature, we have to submerge the bodies in a boiler to thaw them. These bodies are assigned to the tables you saw in the previous room. The families can choose to receive an urn after we cremate the parts we don't use. The crematorium is on the fourth level.

The second level is where the skins are mounted. Rows of off-white muscled mannequins with hollow eye sockets pose: saluting, lying in sniper position, standing in shooting position, throwing grenades, crouching, running.

Next to each mannequin is a short grey cabinet with shallow drawers. She slides out the top drawer: Egg crate grey foam nests glass eyes. Pairs of brown, black, blue, and green irises. Next drawer: Eyebrows and eyelashes, shades of brown, black, and blond. Next drawer: Glove-like silicone hands with plastic fingernails.

I thought the hands were real skin when I saw that one guy in the lobby. Well that's the point, she says. But no, it's pretty difficult to remove the skin from hands, and then mount it. Plus, by using silicone, it's easier to position the hands around a trigger, tossing a grenade, saluting, or what have you. She slides the drawer back in place. The fatty parts of the face, like the lips and cheeks, are also filled with silicone. Look here.

We walk to another mounting station. See, Camilla here just filled in the lips with silicone. She looks up, but goes right back to stitching the skin down the back of the head and neck. The brown irises are in the sockets. The lips look naturally full. The rest of the skin is draped around the shoulders.

On the first level the mounted skins are fitted with uniforms. Boots are polished glossy, placed and laced up on the soldiers, sailors, airmen, marines. Their hands are fitted with rifles, handguns (real guns, but defunct). A Navy S.E.A.L has his face painted black and green. A Marine is fitted with a pressed dress uniform, blue pants [black, gold-buttoned coat, left breast lined with medals, white belt] white-gloved hand saluting the black brim of his white cap.

Back out in the dull concrete stairwell, we walk down to the fourth level. Long room, a row of refrigerated body containers on each side, an arched brick crematory at the end. A man stands next to one of the containers tapping a clipboard with a pen. The Lead Taxidermist yells, Patrick, we have our volunteer. We walk closer, my head swivels between the bodies on each wall. Would you mind terribly if he watched the start of the process? Not at all, Patrick says, as long as he doesn't mind helping lift the cadaver onto the stretcher. Do you mind? No, I say.

Grasp the other end of the sheet, Patrick says. The cold yellow toenails scrape my wrist. Patrick grins. The flesh had been removed from the head and upper body, revealing grey muscle. But the flesh was still attached from forearms to fingertips. And from hips to toes. Flesh still attached to penis, a smooth line cut around the pubic hair.

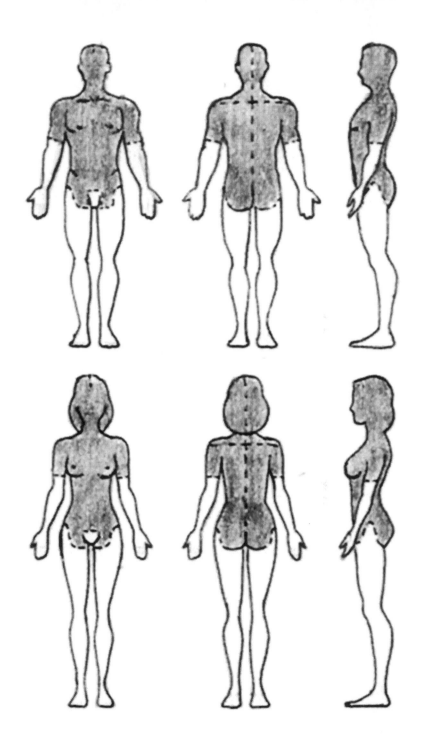

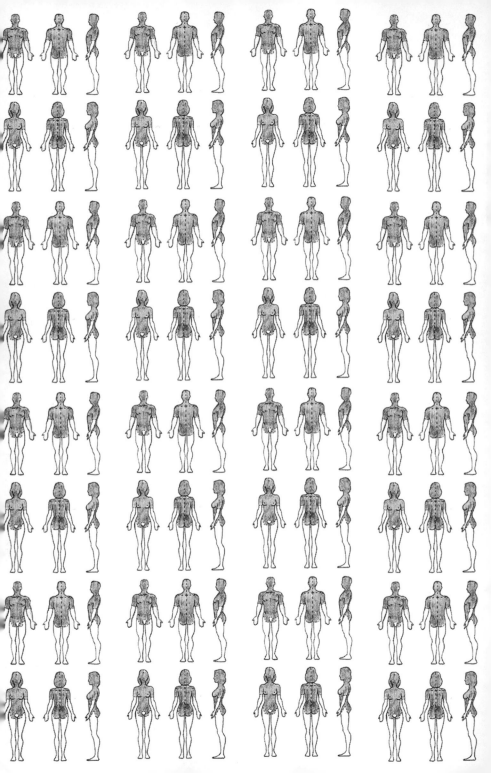

Subject Interview #02187

I am supposed to meet a veteran at his house so he can show me photos from Iraq. He's told me before that it's difficult for him to look at the pictures. I've been waiting for two years. But now he wants to do it "as soon as fucking possible." He leaves next week to go on a VA sponsored, two-month intensive therapy residency because, "Shit is getting worse, the meds aren't helping, so hopefully seven hours of therapy six days a week for two months will help." I tell him I can wait until he gets back. "Let's do it now," he says, "because this shit haunts me and I don't want them in my house, and I agree with my wife that I shouldn't look at these photos ever again after I come back."

At his house, we sit on the couch. His Rottweiler and Black Lab lay at his feet. They follow him while he plugs an external hard drive full of photos into his 65" television.

"So this here, is when we had to leave Al Asad Airbase in a convoy, just to deliver this Suburban to a Colonel."

"This is just some stuff on the side as we're rolling along."

"We're on the back side of Abu Ghraib prison, and you see that little kid off the right hand side?"

"You'll notice, all the other little kids are playing on the left hand side of the road. So that immediately tells us there's something wrong. Well what it was is right up the road his family was dead. They killed his whole family out in the middle of the road."

"Who killed his whole family?"

"I don't know. But it was my call, if we were gonna stop the convoy and pick the kid up or not. And I left the kid. We just kept rolling, till we left him. I left him. So that's one of those things you know, a collateral thing, you don't think you'd ever have to make a decision like that. But just for delivering that fucking Suburban to a Colonel...I, I, get stuck with fucking nightmares the rest of my life."

"Fuck"

"You notice how you never see any little girls?"

"Oh yeah."

"Cuz all the little girls are out in the wadis, working."

"What are the wadis?"

"It's just wherever they grow whatever their staple is there. They're out there working."

"And the boys are playing?"

"And the boys are playing, the boys are going to school, they're learning how to build bombs.   Even now I freeze up whenever I see a little boy standing on the side of the road."

"Suburban delivered intact."

"Good for the Colonel, I guess."

"Whatever.   You want some more water?"

"I'm good, thanks though."

"I would offer you a beer, but I had to quit drinking a long time ago."

"Yeah, I remember you telling me that. Good for you."

"So how are you doing with your drinking?"

*"I don't know, man. Sometimes I over-do it, but, you know . . .
not too bad I guess."*

"Sounds like what I used to tell myself.   I'm not trying
to be a dick though, just letting you know, if you need help,
get it."

"Yeah."

"Aww, here are some of the pups, eating a cow."

"You told me about the dogs a while back, but didn't go into detail."

"Well, I think all the dogs over there are strays. The Iraqis don't care about 'em, they treat dogs like shit. And we were ordered to shoot the dogs on sight."

"What the fuck for?"

"Cuz, they'd bark and give us away. But I know I didn't go to Iraq to shoot no fuckin' dogs."

"Do you still have the pictures of the dead dogs?"

"No. I deleted them. But it's pointless, because I can't unsee piles and piles of dead dogs on the side of the road. You don't wanna see that shit anyway."

"So how does that work with your therapy dogs? Does it fuck up your relationship at all?"

"I mean, it's something I think about a lot, but my pups make me feel a whole helluva lot better. I don't know, I guess it's like atonement or something, me taking care of my pups, but they really take care of me, so I don't know. I really don't know."

U.S. State Department on Terrorism:

Terrorists almost always act with a specific objective in mind. They are very dedicated and willing to make great sacrifices to be successful. Generally they are well trained, often with a military or paramilitary background. Many groups are also well funded and well equipped.

They conduct surveillance activities to gather information on potential targets, sometimes for weeks or months before acting. Not only do terrorists plan their attacks in great detail, they also rehearse their operations.

Many terrorists are willing to die for their beliefs, and this factor alone makes them extremely dangerous.

I start running to my Commander's office. Sir, I say, I'd like to report someone for terrorist activities. Who would you like to report, he says. Myself, I say. My goddamn self. Ohh I see, he says, You've got your definitions mixed up again.

fallen [faw-luh n]

verb

1. past participle of fall.

adjective

2. having dropped or come down from a higher place, from an upright position, or from a higher level, degree, amount, quality, value, number, etc.

3. having lost your chastity; "a fallen woman"

synonyms: dishonored, lost, loose, shamed, ruined, disgraced, immoral, sinful, unchaste

4. killed in battle; "fallen soldiers"

synonyms: lost, dead, slaughtered, slain, perished, massacred, murdered

hero [hi(ə)rō]

noun

1. a person, typically a man, who is admired or idealized for courage, outstanding achievements, or noble qualities

synonyms: brave person, brave man/woman, man/woman of courage, man/woman of the hour, lion heart, warrior, knight; champion, victor, conqueror

adjective

2. [North American]: another term for submarine sandwich

fr. Greek heros: an immortal being; demigod.

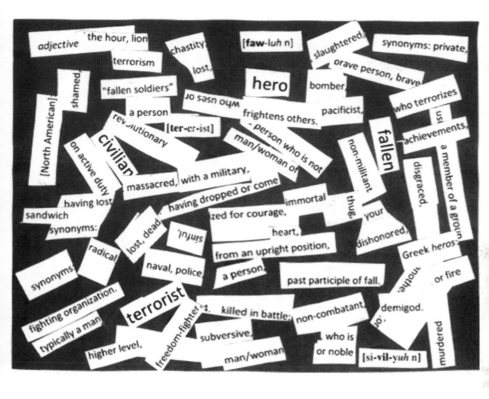

civilian [si-vil-yuh n]

noun

1. a person who is not on active duty with a military, naval, police, or fire fighting organization.

2. Informal. Anyone regarded by members of a profession, interest group, society, etc., as not belonging; non-professional; outsider.

synonyms: private, non-combatant, pacificist, non-militant

terrorist [ter-er-ist]

noun

1. a person, usually a member of a group, who uses or advocates terrorism

2. a person who terrorizes or frightens others.

synonyms: freedom-fighter, subversive, bomber, thug, radical, rebel, revolutionary

Field Notes

I was researching the television coverage of the Vietnam War, comparing it to the coverage of the current war(s).

I was watching the Vietnam War footage on my laptop, muted. But my television was on, some sitcom playing, the words low but the laugh-track loud.

Soldiers hop out of a helicopter ducking as they run off
HaHaHaHaHa

Soldier burying infant
HaHaHaHaHa

Shooting Viet Cong prisoner in the head
HaHaHaHaHa

Families running down the street, little girl naked, crying
HaHaHaHaHa

[… *switching to television coverage of the current war(s).*]

News anchor looking serious. Cut to: American flag waving
HaHaHaHaHa

Soldiers helping pull down a statue

Cut to: soldiers kicking in door
HaHaHaHaHa

The horrors of war entered the living rooms of Americans for the first time during the Vietnam War.

Sitcoms use laugh tracks to make the audience at home feel like they are part of a bigger crowd, like sitting in a movie theater or comedy club.

Many Vietnam veterans and scholars feel that the uncensored and overly negative television coverage helped turn the American public against the war, and against the veterans themselves.

"We're much more likely to laugh at something funny in the presence of other people," says Bill Kelley, a psychology professor at Dartmouth College.

Vietnam was a lesson. The television coverage of the current war(s) is *not* overly negative and uncensored. The horrors of war are still there, but not here, in our living rooms. We can celebrate, laugh.

"In other countries, the business of laughter is left to the viewers."—Jean Baudrillard, *America*

Observation

In the military we watch a lot of movies about ourselves. I've seen *Top Gun* far too many times. *Hunt for Red October. Saving Private Ryan, Tora! Tora! Tora!* War movie after war movie. Eventually we start acting like the actors in those films. Which is why, admittedly, I get a bit defensive when I watch military films with civilians and they say the films are inauthentic and cliché. And I'm like, "Hey, we act cliché in real life too."

We are obsessed with the Hollywood versions of ourselves. The CNN version. The FOX version. You know how many people idolize that abusive drill sergeant from *Full Metal Jacket*? Or does the film idolize actual abusive drill sergeants?

We are the live wires. It is difficult to know where the circuit begins. Did we start acting like the movies or the movies started acting like us or both influenced each other or both are lying to themselves about our image, which is reduced to a few types: ruff-n-tuff, hard-lovin' yet tender, hard-drinkin' barely intelligent robotic super patriotic heroic defender of everything good. True, there are those caricatures. But we are also apathetic, ashamed, terrified, un-patriotic, vulnerable, anti-heroic, math geniuses, dope-dealers, preachers, coke-sniffers, painters, wife-beaters, pedophiles, stand-up cats, and no-good motherfuckers.

Field Notes On Submarine Space

Atmosphere defined: a conventional unit of pressure. Below are some units of pressure for nuclear submarines.

Oxygen

Earth's normal atmospheric oxygen level is 21%. A submarine's normal atmospheric oxygen level is 17%. Along with fatigue, low oxygen can lead to temporarily reduced brain function.

Men

Men huddled at a table bickering about someone who eats too loudly.

Men huddled in the engine room smoking cigarettes. It's legal, and safe.

Men huddled around a laptop watching porn and cheering on the man.

Men gossiping about whose wives are cheating.

Where are the women? I've never seen any official rules, but a lot of dudes say it's because women bicker and gossip too much. They are emotional and moody. It is not good for women and men to be in such close quarters because the women will distract the men. Women are unsanitary because their sanitary napkins will clog the sewage pipes.

Bodies

Penises are often the center of attention. As evident by the amount of men who display their penises in creative positions, such as the "Squirrel on a Trampoline." He stretches his scrotum and bounces his penis up and down.

Two men, one displaying the 'Squirrel', and the other the 'Hot Dog', face each other at opposite ends of an aisle. Other men are cheering, "Aww, he's got the squirrel, man. That's hard to beat." The two men hop toward each other, switching penis positions, saying "Take that, fag."

They continue to hop. The switching grows more frantic. Until their penises touch. Mouths are open. Eyes are wide. The man with the squirrel says, "Eww, you fuckin' faggot."

The crowd chants, "Faggot, faggot!"

Sanitation

Toilets

In a tiny metal stall, a 5-inch wide pipe runs below a metal toilet. Turn a valve to release the water, fill the bowl, then pull a large lever that opens another valve, and your waste is carried to a large tank where it is stored until emptied.

Showers

Also serving as what some call a "masturbatorium." When you wedge into this metal shower, there is often soap scum and semen floating in the bottom. Recommended shower time is 2-3 minutes to save water. Wet yourself, turn the water off, lather, and rinse. This soapy semen water is also collected in the storage tank.

Blowing Sanitaries (Sans)

Once the tank is full of everyone's excrement, urine, semen, and dishwater, it has to be emptied, usually once a week. This mixture is shot out of the submarine with 1000 pounds of pressure. I imagine a whale with diarrhea. During the 'Blowing of the Sans' you are not supposed to use the bathrooms because if you open that valve. That's why there's a big red sign on the stalls that read

BLOWING SANS
DO NOT FLUSH

A first-time sub rider awoke and stumbled to the bathroom, not seeing the signs. He pulled the lever. A geyser of shit shot up into his face, knocked him down. We found him lying on the floor flooded with feces. He said, "It looked like a claw of shit reached up and grabbed my face." They cleaned everyone's waste from his mouth and underneath his eyelids.

Trash Removal

Garbage is collected from around the sub and consolidated by using a trash compactor and placed in cans 28 inches long and 9 inches in diameter. 30 pounds of lead weights are added to make sure the cans will sink once they are shot out of the submarine. About 30 cans are shot out once a week. Multiply that number times 52 weeks a year, per 72 submarines in the fleet, for let's say, 1 year.

1 year, 1 sub = 1,560 cans (give or take a few hundred to account for down time). 1 year, 72 subs = 112,320 cans. 20 years, 72 subs = 2,246,400 cans of garbage at the bottom of the ocean.

Beds/ Food /Time

Time is marked by shifts of work/sleep and meals. My schedule was 12 hours on and 12 off, up to 120 days with no holidays or vacations. Since I wasn't a permanent crewmember and only came aboard for special missions, my team was extra people and there weren't enough beds for us. Therefore, makeshift beds were made in the Torpedo Room, next to torpedoes.

Beds (Racks)

2 feet wide and 6 feet long. Stacked three high, with only a forearm's length of overhead room. Imagine a coffin.

Comparison: Minimum requirements for prison bunks are 3 inches wider, 5 inches longer, with at least 3 more feet of overhead room.

A 4-inch deep pan underneath, called a *coffin locker*, is where you must store all of your belongings for the next 3-4 months. This space is shared by two people. So is your bed. Sharing your bed is called *hot racking*, because the bed is still warm from body heat when it's your turn to sleep. So while I'm at work for 12 hours my 'bunkmate' sleeps and farts in our bed and vice versa.

Food

Four meals a day, every six hours, breakfast, lunch, dinner, and *midrats* (midnight rations). Midrats: a culmination of the previous three meals. "Tonight's soup is Macaroni Diced Ham with a side of pancakes." Towards the end there's a shortage of food. The last four days was nothing but PB & J sandwiches and frozen shrimp for all meals, with a few pancakes. This was because of a time extension.

Time

A good working ratio of sub time in weeks to normal time is 1:3. Therefore, when we receive messages that say, "Something important happened, you've been extended for three weeks." Those three weeks feel like nine. Some want to get home to their wives and children. Some want to get home because they know their wives are cheating. Some want to get to port to visit Lui Yang, their favorite Thai prostitute. Some want to get to their wives *and* Lui Yang. Some return with their bank accounts emptied and wives moved out of state. Some are missing the births of their children and the deaths of family members. I called my mom from Japan, she said, "By the way, your aunt died a few months ago. The funeral was nice."

Thresholds ---> Tipping Points

Thermoluminescent Dosimeter (TLD)

A chapstick-sized black plastic tube with a grey cap. A slot to slide your belt through. Must be worn at all times in order to get an accurate read on your personal ionizing radiation exposure by measuring the intensity of visible light emitted from the crystal within. Often the TLD slips off and falls into a crack. There's a mad scramble to retrieve it. Once a month we line up, TLD in hand, and the radiation expert measures our exposure. Safe for now.

Oxygen Candles

When the O2 levels dip below 15%, Oxygen Candles must be burned so we don't get terribly sleepy or die. The cans cylinder, 6-inch diameter, knee length height. I don't know what chemicals are in the cylinder, but the burning leaves cake-like ash. The canisters line the passageways, smoldering, producing oxygen. Put my nose close to the ash, hoping I can breathe.

Notes to Self About Thresholds

You can't go anywhere—accept it.

Have a ritual, like drinking green tea, or the airplane bottles of whiskey you snuck onboard. Read Kurt Vonnegut's *Slaughterhouse-Five* as a reminder that: You *are* unstuck in time in a human zoo.

Systematically lower your expectation/emotional level over time so that disappointment is tolerable. So if, at Week 14, you get a *Time Extension*, you won't cry in the corner like you did last time. At Week 16 or greater. Don't expect shit. Don't feel shit.

We finally get off the sub. In the middle of the ocean because our mission is done and the sub has to get back to business. We climb down the sub into a little boat. Waves splash inside the boat. The little boat takes us to a ship. We climb up the side of the ship. We wait on the ship for two hours. A helicopter takes us to base. We wait on base for an hour until a cab takes us to a hotel.

One of the submariners is being medically discharged from sub duty because he needed a Psychological Evaluation. For 4 months he dribbled an imaginary basketball around and never spoke to anyone. During his Evaluation he spun the ball on his index finger and shot hook shots. When we got off, he passed the ball to someone else. He didn't need it any longer.

In the hotel bar, I hear him speak for the first time. He says, "See, it takes a lot of stupid maneuvers just to get back to normal life."

Possible Stories to Include*

I was pissed in Anger Management after the therapist suggested that my parents' relationship model is possibly the reason why I thought it was acceptable to hit my wife back.

My Chief was mad because I was dating a girl we worked with that he was in love with.

I got in trouble for dropping a girl off on base after we'd been out drinking. She forgot to turn on her headlights and got a DUI.

My Chief had three kids and his wife was overweight. So he had another young girlfriend. I don't understand why he was upset with me.

"It is acceptable. She shouldn't have hit me in the first place!"

When I saw her get pulled over I sped off base.

I knew the therapist was right.

I called her while the cops were checking her I.D and told her not to mention I dropped her off, keep my name out of it. She couldn't of course.

My Chief was also mad about another girl I was dating. He told me that I was hogging the pussy.

"Well, I didn't hit her *back*, exactly. She stabbed me in the hand with a butcher knife, which is equivalent to, or greater than hitting, *then* I hit her."

I dislike the coupling of hogs and pussy to form a metaphor.

For the following three months, my command made me give weekly Alcohol & Safety training because of my irresponsible actions.

"So I'm not supposed to hit someone if they stab me??"

My Chief told me he just asked this girl for some pussy and she said, "Hell yeah I've been waiting for you to ask." Five minutes later the girl walked over and said, "Sorry Chief, I can't help you with that." It is unclear what she couldn't help him with. But he did have the embarrassed looked of rejection and of someone who got caught in a lie.

Since my friend got a DUI, she wasn't allowed to drive on base anymore. My Chief volunteered to drive her off base to her car. She said he would take his shirt off and flex while they waited for his car to warm up.

"She shouldn't have had sex with my friend in my house while my kid was upstairs sleeping."

My Chief's other girlfriend was cheating on him with another Chief. My Chief and the other Chief got into a fight in a grocery store parking lot.

During my Alcohol & Safety training I discussed the differences between good whiskey and cheap whiskey.

I am ashamed to write a detailed account of my ex-wife's and my domestic abuse.

In the grocery store parking lot, my Chief got beat up by the other Chief. My Chief filed a subsequent restraining order. He told his wife the other Chief had been harassing him at work over performance evaluations.

I apologized to my friend for speeding off base and trying to bully her into not mentioning my name. She accepted. From then on we did collaborative Alcohol & Safety training.

Abuse sounds better when preceded by 'domestic'. It sounds tamed. Tamed Abuse.

I realized I'm talking shit about my Chief for a couple of reasons. 1. He's lower than a slug's asshole. 2. Which makes me feel better about myself for hitting my ex-wife.

My friend and I still go out drinking. And we're safe about it, I guess. We get fucked up and talk shit about my Chief. She's thinking of filing a sexual harassment charge against him.

I've also just realized that me saying I "hit" my ex-wife is a copout. I want to blame the military for making me so euphemistic. But it's not true. I'm too embarrassed to say I punched her in the ribs.

I'm tired of talking about my Chief. I'm being petty. Because I'm still bitter because he used his Chief power to demote me for insubordination.

My friend never filed that sexual harassment charge. She was afraid she'd have some Chief power used against her.

The older woman who I was cheating on my ex-wife with would have never stabbed me.

My Chief told me in private that he and I both knew what my first acts of insubordination were, "Fucking the broad I love, and not sharing." Everyone knows what my final act of insubordination was: Throwing a chair at him in front of everyone.

Once again I'm evading any real responsibility. I just moved on from cheating on my ex-wife to talking about my Chief.

This guy at work killed himself because he didn't' wanna go back out to sea.

Not my Chief though. Maybe he'll get killed in Afghanistan or something.

No, that would suck for his wife and kids, and his other two girlfriends.

It's time to stop writing when I realize that my Chief and I are similar. Except that I won't get killed in Afghanistan. Because I refuse to go. Ain't none of them folks over there ever did anything to me.

---

* Don't inlcude any of these stories.

Subject Interview #00080

I work for the VA as a Legal Administrative Specialist. I can't give you specific details because I'm sworn to confidentiality.

Of course, totally understand.

So I handle different issues that veterans may have. But I often come across veterans who've been raped while on active duty.

I've read the statistics, but even with us being in, it's not something you really hear about.

People would be amazed at how often women and men are being raped in the military. I myself was raped by a fellow veteran, not while on Active Duty but we both were veterans. And what's even more astonishing is what the women are being told. It's as if the military has a script to read to rape victims once they report their rapes. *If* they report their rapes. In one day, I spoke to two rape victims, *two*. And they both were told the same things, "What did they expect when they joined the military and why would they ruin someone's career with lies?"

The next day, I spoke with another rape victim, she said something that really hurt my heart, "I never thought I would've gotten pregnant by the man that raped me." I'm not sure what became of the pregnancy because it was too personal. But I wanted to reach out and hug her. The girl suffered from PTSD and depression from the military sexual trauma. But the VA said her depression wasn't connected to her rape. Sadly, all three women suffered from PTSD. And just by talking with them, even I could tell that it was connected to rape.

These three women had so much in common: The main thing was that they were looking for validation. For someone to acknowledge what happened to them and to tell them that they weren't at fault and that they weren't victims, they were survivors. Because the military never acknowledged their pain. They never told them that it wasn't their fault and they never assured them that they were protected. These women were made to feel as though these predators' careers meant more than the women. They were made to feel as though they brought it on themselves by joining. One woman said that she was told, "Why would a woman so beautiful join an organization with all men unless she wanted to be raped?"

And that was just two days. My first veteran that suffered from Military Sexual Trauma was a man. He said he'd been raped by men in boot camp. He said that he was told to leave and not come back after spending four weeks in the military. He went into grave detail as to what happened to him. I don't wanna go back into those details. But he said it happened on multiple occasions and no one was held accountable. And just like the women, he was told that he would ruin soldiers' careers.

Brief History: Tailhook Scandal

What is Tailhook?

The Tailhook Association is a private organization comprised of Active Duty, Reserve, and Retired Navy and Marine Corps aviators, defense contractors, and others. The name "tailhook" comes from the device that halts aircraft when they land on aircraft carriers. The Tailhook Association has a host of corporate sponsors, including Raytheon, Rolls Royce, G.E., USAA, and MBDA Missile Systems. The Tailhook Association hosts annual symposiums designed "to contribute to the enhancement of professionalism, camaraderie, and morale among carrier and other sea-based aviators."

September 1991

The 35th Annual Tailhook Symposium was held at the Las Vegas Hilton Hotel. This symposium was special: It focused on the aviation heroes of the U.S. Navy and Marine Corps in Operation Desert Storm. The symposium had 4,000 attendees. This was the largest meeting yet held. At the three-day symposium, 83 women and 7 men reported that they were sexually assaulted. Lieutenant Gary Mandich, one of the many alleged participants in the sexual assault, told media: "Everyone needs to seriously lighten up. What do they expect? This is Vegas baby! They call this symposium 'Tail' hook for a reason!"

April 1992

Investigators for the DOD interviewed 2,900 people who attended Tailhook '91 and obtained photographs, documents and other evidence of crimes and misconduct by naval aviators. The Inspector General and the Naval Investigative Service issued a 2,000-page report detailing scenes where dozens of women were sexually harassed and assaulted.

Rear Admiral Duvall M. Williams Jr. and his team led the investigation, and concluded that the incident was mainly the fault of low-ranked enlisted men "behaving poorly." Assistant Secretary of the Navy, Barbara S. Pope, refused to accept the results of the investigation, especially after Rear Admiral Williams said, in Barbara Pope's presence, "a lot of female Navy pilots are go-go dancers, topless dancers, or hookers."

When RADM Williams issued his final report, finding no senior Navy officials at fault, Pope told the United States Secretary of the Navy that she would resign if the Navy did not "do another report and look at what we needed to do about accountability and responsibility and the larger issues at hand."

August 1992

Because of the Navy's 2,000-page report, in addition to Barbara Pope's insistence, the Pentagon's Inspector General launched a set of new investigations.

September 1992

The Pentagon's Inspector General issued a critical report on the Navy's first investigation, saying that senior Navy officials deliberately ignored the participation of senior officers at Tailhook and undermined their own investigation to avoid bad publicity.

April 1993

The Pentagon's Inspector General released a second report stating that the investigative files of at least 140 officers were being referred to the military services for possible disciplinary action for indecent exposure, assault, conduct unbecoming of an officer, and lying to Pentagon investigators under oath.

Some Incidents at Tailhook

The Gauntlet

The Gauntlet was where the most documented assaults occurred. The Gauntlet was a group of up to two hundred men who lined the corridor outside the hospitality suites around 10:30 each night. The men "touched" women who passed down the corridor. The touching ranged from consensual pats on the breasts and buttocks to violent grabbing, groping, clothes-stripping, and other assaultive behavior.

The men would start by pounding the walls and chanting "gauntlet, gauntlet," as women walked down the hallway.

Military code words such as "clear deck," "foul deck," "wave off," and "bolter," were used to orchestrate group behavior. For example "wave off" was used to indicate the approach of an unattractive woman, and the men would respond by turning away from her. Often one individual acted as "master of ceremonies" whose duty it was to coax women to walk down the corridor, sometimes even picking them up on his shoulder and carrying them into the crowd. The DoD investigation reported that many women "freely and knowingly" participated in the gauntlet. The gauntlet had become a tradition at Tailhook symposia, as indicated by it being printed on T-shirts and worn by attendees.

Pool Area

Several witnesses reported individuals walking around naked and streaking in the pool patio area. One female student from the University of Nevada at Las Vegas was talking with friends on the patio when a sheet of glass from one of the upper floor windows was pushed out. She suffered a concussion from glass shards striking her head. The glass was pushed out by service members who were pressing their bare buttocks on the window while "mooning" the crowd below.

VAW-110: The "Leg-shaving Suite"

Carrier Airborne Squadron. San Diego, CA
Hilton Suite: 303
Commanding Officer: CDR Christopher Remshak
    (attended Tailhook '91)
Squadron Members Attending: Approximately 50
Type of Alcohol Served: Beer, Mixed Drinks
Total Cost of Alcohol: $900
Total Cost of Room Damage: $1,316

The VAW-110 suite's feature attraction was the "leg shaving booth." Using hot towels and baby oil, two male squadron members at a time would shave the legs, and in some cases the pubic areas, of female squadron members and civilian females. A large banner reading "Free Leg Shaves!" hung from the sliding glass door, which permitted onlookers from the pool area to watch. Some male officers from the suite reportedly licked legs to ensure "quality control." Most participants claimed to have not been forced, but one female Navy officer and another woman reported being badgered into taking part.

VMFMP-3 "The Rhino Suite"

Marine Corps Tactical Reconnaissance Squadron
(Deactivated 1990)
Hilton Suite: 308
Commanding Officer: N/A
Squadron Members Attending: Unable to determine
Type of Alcohol Served: Beer, "Rhino Spunk"
Total Cost of Alcohol: Unable to determine
Total Cost of Suite Damage: $530

The VMFP-3 suite was called the "Rhino" room after the squadron mascot. Suite activities centered around a hand painted mural of a rhinoceros (approximately 5' x 8') to which was affixed a dildo rigged by squadron members for use as a drink dispensing mechanism. The dildo dispensed an alcoholic based liquid referred to as "Rhino Spunk" (rum, Kahlua, milk/cream and ice).

Squadron members stated that women were not "forced, co-erced, or intimidated in any way to drink from the dildo." However, during the course of the investigation, five women reported being physically restrained when they refused to drink, as aviators chanted or verbally harassed them.

Yes, the Tailhook Scandal is sensational. But sexual assault and its cover-up by leadership aren't exceptions, it happens frequently. The Navy and the Pentagon knew this. So like Barbara Pope insisted, they "looked at what we needed to do about accountability and responsibility and the larger issues at hand." Thus, the Navy and the DoD created task forces that developed a "comprehensive handbook with the goal to educate its members to understand and ulti-mately prevent sexual assault." Navy officials were proud of what they called their "sound bite, bumper sticker ap-proach" to sexual assault."

Participation

Our Chief calls us into the conference room for a GMT (General Military Training) on Sexual Assault. The Training Petty Officer turns on the projector. People groan. "I know, I know," he says, "just suck it up and listen, we only have to do this once a year."

Sexual Assault Prevention & Response

TOGETHER WE CAN PREVENT SEXUAL ASSAULTS

What You Will Learn

* Green Light Behavior
*

* Red Light Behavior
* **Scenarios to stimulate discussion and thought**

Green Light

* **Not sexual harassment:**
* Performance counseling
* Touching which could not be reasonably perceived in a sexual way (such as touching someone on the elbow)
* Counseling on military appearance,
* Social interaction, showing concern, encouragement
* A polite compliment, or friendly conversation.

Yellow Light

Some people could reasonably view these behaviors as unwelcome, and they **could become sexual harassment:**

* Violating personal "space"
* Whistling, questions about personal life, lewd or sexually suggestive comments
* Suggestive posters or calendars, off-color jokes, leering, staring, repeated requests for dates, foul language
* Unwanted letters or poems, sexually suggestive touching, or sitting or gesturing sexually

Red Light

* These behaviors are **always considered sexual harassment:**
* Sexual favors in return for employment rewards, job-related threats if sexual favors are not provided
* Sexually explicit pictures (including calendars or posters) or remarks, using status to request dates, or obscene letters or comments
* The most severe forms of sexual harassment constitute such independently criminal conduct as sexual assault.

Scenario

A female ENS [ensign] at a large shore command regularly encountered a male LT [lieutenant] from another department in the passageway. On two occasions, the LT grabbed the ENS around the waist and pulled her close to him, although he did not say anything of a sexual nature.

The ENS was upset and both times she told the LT his conduct was offensive and not to touch her again. Nonetheless, the LT repeated the behavior a third time. The ENS became angry and threatened to "feed the LT her fist" if he touched her again. A LCDR [lieutenant commander] overheard the exchange and reprimanded the ENS for being disrespectful to a senior officer.

Questions

- Is this behavior appropriate?
- Is confronting the behavior right?
- Is the LT entitled to one "mistake"?
- What actions should each party take?
- What type of behavior is this?
  - a.) Green
  - b.) Yellow
  - c.) Red

Discussion

- The LT's behavior was inappropriate.
- Lack of verbal comments of a sexual nature is irrelevant -- the **behavior** was of a sexual nature.
- The ENS's attempt to informally resolve the conflict directly with the LT in two prior occasions was entirely appropriate (although she was not required to wait until the "third strike" to inform her chain of command).
- Yes, this is an example of Red Light Behavior.

"Any additional questions or comments?"

Someone in the front raises his hand, "Yeah, I disagree with that being red light behavior. I think it's yellow, because his actions could have become sexual harassment. And—"

"No," another guy interrupts, "that's definitely red light behavior. But we all know, if you sit at a red light long enough, it'll eventually turn green."

Everyone laughs.

Observation

We already know what happened, but everyone can't stop talking about it in the smoke shack. One of our Chiefs got caught, through his work email, fraternizing with four young female seamen, fucking them, giving them money, showing favoritism at work, threatening other girls who didn't want to fuck him, all the usual stuff. The girls got kicked out, dishonorable discharge, nothing happens to the Chief, he's still a Chief (it takes an act of congress to demote a Chief), his wife didn't divorce him, all the usual stuff.

But this thing is only the first brick of a storied house that everyone builds in the space of a smoke break.

You think that's something, someone says, when I was on the carrier this one bitch got busted for running a prostitution ring. She made like a hundred grand on a six-month deployment.

Another guy says, That ain't shit, this Master Chief at my last command was fucking the C.O, and that broad was fucking another C.O. at another command, and he was fucking with seamen and ended up giving the other C.O. herpes, and she wound up giving the Master Chief herpes.

Oh yeah, another guy says, this dude I was on the ship with went AWOL in the Philippines, he started out with only three bitches. Now he got a whole fleet of hoes. And you know whenever I go to the P.I., he gives me hoes for free, like three of 'em for the whole weekend.

That's like that one guy in Japan, someone else says, the one who was pimping out those teenage Japanese girls. One of the girls didn't pay him so he stabbed her in the neck with a screwdriver and threw her out the window of the fifth floor.

Yeah man, someone else says, remember that one Master Chief who was sneaking cocaine on the sub and bringing it back to the states?

What about that guy who smashed his wrist with a hammer because he didn't wanna go back on the sub?

Yeah, but that's not as bad as that dude who hanged himself in his closet right after he got off the sub.[7]

I put out my third cigarette and walk away. At their next command, the Chief now, whose recent bust started this conversation, will end up being their Best Worst Story.

---

* I knew the guy who hanged himself. They kept sending him out, so his wife would go back home whenever he deployed. He'd be back for a week, gone again for a few months, back for a week, gone again. His wife was on her way back to Hawaii, and he was supposed to pick her up from the airport. She took a cab home and found him hanging in the closet. For his 21st birthday, he and his wife had planned to go on a cruise. She said she was moving back to Kansas and never wanted to see the fucking ocean again.

<u>Observation</u>

I forgot what we're fighting for

We are heroes

Bearing. Mark. Bearing zero-four-seven

Oh, does your little pussy hurt, need a tampon

Man, we've been out here way too long

Bearing. Mark. Bearing two-seven-three

You knew what you signed up for, we all took that oath

She cheated on you last time we were out to sea

in a fucking tin can floating under the ocean

ksssh We really don't know where *kssssh*

Bearing. Mark. Bearing zero-nine-four

You know what we're fighting for dumbass

nuke that godforsaken place off the map

ksssh kssssh biiiiii camel jockeys *eeeeeeee*

I want some pussy when we get to port

No sir, that signal is not a threat

Yeah, save us all some trouble, nuke it

Subject Interview # 11067

We were in Afghanistan, patrolling the perimeter of the base, seven of us, just doing our normal security rounds. We'd done this every day for the last, I don't know, maybe seven months or so, and it was always quiet. So we were just kinda joking around, not a big deal, then click. My best friend stepped on a landmine. Blood and bits of flesh splattered us. Some even flew into my mouth.

I can't eat meat anymore.

Subject Interview #00023

Let me get this straight ... you're studying us like we're some kind of zoo animals or something? But you're in the zoo like the rest of us. Have you ever seen a monkey doing a study on other monkeys in the same cage?

But I don't feel like I'm in the same cage. Well maybe sometimes...

And that's where you're wrong. You're just like the rest of us, doing the same things, subjected to all the same bullshit, everything. Good luck with the book though.

Can I put this interview in the book?

If that's what you wanna call it, an interview.

Field Notes

Five more Taxidermy Museums of Military Heroes have opened across the United States.

Because of my "years of commitment to volunteer service" at the first Taxidermy Museum, my command is sending me to the ribbon-cutting ceremony at the largest one. Which is next to Arlington National Cemetery. And Arlington recently ran out of ground space, so no one will be buried there any longer.

"But there are still options for our fallen to be *in* Arlington," says a White House Public Relations Official at the ceremony. "And there are plans to open five more Taxidermy Museums within the next ten years."

The current president, and the two previous presidents nod in agreement. The current president cuts the big red ribbon with gold, over-sized scissors. An old black lady next to me says she's happy she lived to see a black president. She asks me am I happy. I say yes.

But I don't tell her that I'm also kinda sad, because I'd always been happy that black people had never been the face of fucking people up overseas. I mean, we've fucked people up overseas just by being in the military, but, I don't know, it's different now.

I keep all of that to myself when the president gives me my Naval Achievement Medal for my years of volunteer service. I smile and shake his hand like nothing is wrong.

The option to still be in Arlington, was to engrave service members' names on bronze tabs and tack them to benches. All of the roads in the cemetery are lined with benches. The space under the benches are packed with flowers, some real and wilted, and some plastic and colorful.

I fell asleep snuggled in my pea coat on one the benches with my friend's name on it. There were forty-nine other names on there too. I was awakened by a snot-nosed kid. His brown mittens hold a dozen of white plastic calla lilies. His dad stands behind him holding an urn. The boy says, "Excuse me mister, my mother's name is on this bench."

A homeless man on the bench to our right says he is glad they woke me up instead because he's tired of people waking him up just to look at a goddamn name. He gets up and walks across the road and sits with his friends on another bench because he said the father was crying too much.

A couple of neighborhoods had been torn down to make space for the museum. Now the cemetery is having problems with homeless people sleeping on the benches and using the garbage cans for fires.

On the way out I toss my medal into one of the burning garbage cans.

And one of the workers carries a box to one of the benches with no names on it. He pulls out a bronze tab, fogs it with his breath, and polishes it with a white cloth before tapping it into place with a rubber mallet. He does this each time until the bench is filled.

Participation #24780

```
static grey monitor\\: black
crosshairs

infrared: redorange body heat moving
out\\inside house

grip joystick. fleshpad of thumb :
red button \\\ Whiteflash
```

Job well done, his superiors tell him. He takes off his glasses and rubs his eyes. Avoids seeing the smoke clear.

Shift change: Places notes and the coordinates inside safe, spins dial. Logs off workstation. Passes down activities of previous shift. His replacement tells him, You're lucky.

In the four-lane highway bumper-to-bumper, license plate numbers arrange themselves into coordinates: 48' 20N 71° 28'E. He winces at the low-flying airplanes arriving and departing.

He slings his camouflage backpack onto the couch. Unlaces boots in his bedroom, hangs uniform in closet. In the second bedroom of the apartment, he sits at his desk to check email. Whiteflash

Looking for mac & cheese in the cupboard, he finds instead, burlap sacks of cardamom, coriander, turmeric, and basmati rice. Checks the door and windows to see if any are broken. Nothing. Calls the police and tells them that someone, maybe squatters, had entered his home, but nothing was taken, just some things were out of place. On his way to Wendy's, he tosses the burlap sacks into the dumpster. He nibbles the edges of his hamburger, waiting for dark. The numbers and letters on the receipt arrange themselves into coordinates.

Back at the apartment complex, he circles the parking lot and reverses into a spot in the corner, with a direct line of sight to his front door and side windows, cuts off headlights, sinks into seat. Eyes narrowed.

All night. Waiting, watching. No movement.

When the sun rises he walks across the parking lot looking side to side. Unlocks the door peeking over his shoulder. Showers, brushes teeth, laces boots. In the refrigerator for eggs, but finds instead a jar labeled *ghee*. Opens the cupboard. The burlap sacks. He thinks maybe he dozed off, or someone broke in while he was away.

In the four-lane highway bumper-to-bumper, license plate numbers arrange themselves into coordinates: 48' 20N 71° 28'E. He winces at the low-flying airplanes arriving and departing. And stops to get coffee. An old man with a blue Vietnam Veteran hat pays.

Shift change: He receives passdown, which includes papers listing yesterday's blast radius and the amount of high-value targets neutralized. He settles in front of his monitors. Slow. Quiet. No movement in or around the crater from yesterday. Slips the papers underneath the keyboard without reading them.

In the break room, the television is showing Breaking News followed by a map of. He stands in a chair and reaches up to turn off the television.

Shift change: Tells his replacement there is nothing to report.

In the four-lane highway bumper-to-bumper, license plate numbers arrange themselves into coordinates: 48' 20N 71° 28'E. He winces at the low-flying airplanes arriving and departing. And stops for Chinese.

He reverses into the same spot from last night. Finishing an eggroll and wiping the grease on his thighs. He walks across the parking lot looking side to side. Unlocks the door peeking over his shoulder. He walks in and finds fourteen people standing in the living room. Men wearing baggy grey pants under long grey shirts, covered by black vests. Women wearing headscarves of the same color that flare out to the waist, and baggy pants. Children wearing the same.

"Who are you? What are you doing here?"

تم کون وہ اور آپ کو کہیں ایک رہیں کر ہر سے ہیں . ہم کہاں ہیں . اس جگہ
اور سے ہت میں گاؤں اپنے ہم منت کیا . کیا نہیں رہیں جانتے . میں ہت نہیں جانتے . ہم ایک
ہم رہاں ہت گا لگے منت ، اس جگہ پر ... ہم کو نہیں جانتے ہم

"Are you the people who've been breaking into my home?"

تم کون وہ اور آپ کو کہیں ایک رہیں کر ہر سے ہیں . ہم کہاں ہیں . اس جگہ
ہم ایک . ہیں رہیں نہیں جانتے . کیا منت ہم اپنے گاؤں میں ہت سے ہیں
اور ہم رہاں ہت گا لگے منت ، اس جگہ پر ... ہم کو نہیں جانتے . تم
نہیں، ہم میں تورٹ نہیں ایک گا ایک ہے . آپ ہم سے ایک چاہتے ہیں . نہیں
نے ہم سے ایک چاہتے ہیں . کس طرح گھر حاصل کرنے کے لیے نہیں
ہم بتائیں . خدا کی محبت کے لیے کس طرح گھر

MQ-9 Reaper

Manufacturer: General Atomics Aeronautical Systems, Inc.

Armament: AGM-114 Hellfire missiles

Speed: 230 mph

Range: 1,150 miles

Crew: Two (pilot and sensor operator)

The unit also incorporates a laser range finder/designator, which precisely designates targets for employment of laser-guided munitions. The MQ-9 can also employ four laser-guided missiles, Air-to-Ground Missile-114 Hellfire, which possess highly accurate, low-collateral damage, anti-armor and anti-personnel engagement capabilities.

اس جمگ ایک ہے . میم تم نہیں جانتی ہے . کیا میم اپنے گاؤر
میم تھے اوار میم رہای ہے تھے لاگیل اس جگمگ رپ ... میم آپ کو نہیں
جانتے . نہیں، میم ہیں میم توٹ نہیں کیا ایک گی ہے . آپا میم سے ایک چاہتے
نہیں . تم نے میم سکس ایک ہے چارہتے . سکس طرح رھگ چاصل کرنے
کے لیے میم ہیں باتئیی . خدا کی محبت کے لیل سکس طرح رھگ
چاصل کرنے کے لیل ہمارہ مربانی میم ہیں باتئیی.

He pleads with them to leave, if not, he could call the police. Pleads some more, if not, he could call, maybe ICE or somebody, ICE is serious business, they mean it, they really mean it. Pleads more. Tells them he is leaving for a while and when he gets back he hopes they are gone, if not ...

اس جگہ ایک ہے . میں تہ نہیں جانتے . کیا منٹ ہم اپنے گاؤر
میں تھے اوا ہم راہی دھت گالے منٹ ، اس جگہ پر ... ہم آپ کو نہیں
جانتے . نہیں ، میم ہی ٹوٹ نہیں کیا ایک گیا ہے . آپ ہم سے ایک چاہتے
ہہ نہیں . تہ نہ ہم سے ایک چاہتے ہیں . کس طرح گھر حاصل کرنے
کے لیے میم بتائیں . خدا کی محبت کے لیے کس طرح گھر
.حاصل کرنے کے لیے برام مہربانی میم بتائیں

He paces around the parking lot, goes to get in his car, but he's left his keys in the apartment. They are still there. Some sitting on the couch, on the floor, standing against the wall. Quick count for reporting purposes: 4 men, 5 women, 5 children.

Drives around town, thinking, mistakenly running red lights. After running a fourth, a cop pulls him over, sees his uniform, thanks him for his service, and lets him off with a warning. Be careful. Yes, sir. Everything alright. Yes, sir, just kinda zoned out for a second, long day at work.

He keeps driving and ends up at Wal-Mart. Follows his feet inside, past the electronics. To the sporting goods. Picks up four queen size air mattresses. Thinks, fourteen, two people per mattress, I need three more. Four more. Maybe five? Four is good.

At the checkout counter the woman asks if he has family coming in. Huh? Do you have family coming in? Oh, yeah. From where? Pak-P-P-Pennsylvania, from Pennsylvania.

AGM-114 Hellfire

Manufacturer: Boeing, Lockheed Martin

Propulsion: Solid propellant rocket

Speed: Subsonic

Range: 1,150 miles

Crew: Two (pilot and sensor operator)

The unit also incorporates a laser range finder/designator, which precisely designates targets for employment of laser-guided munitions. The MQ-9 can also employ four laser-guided missiles, Air-to-Ground Missile-114 Hellfire, which possess highly accurate, low-collateral damage, anti-armor and anti-personnel engagement capabilities.

Case Report: Dirge

Cups of water doused over the heads of vets pushing through streets for parades. Baptized. Faithfully trying to extinguish fires of Traumatic Stress Disorder. It is not Post. It is Now.

Dear Child,

Your   a.) باپ،

      b.) ورور

      c.) بهاﺋی

      d.) ماموں،. was suspected of terrorist activities.

Clear skies.

Grey bird chirp.

That was the last time you _____ with your family.

Celebrate our accuracy.

Sincerely.

.   .   . .   .

b   l   o   w   n   t o   . . b   .   .
            .   .   .   i   .   t

                    .   s   s   s   .

.   .

        .   .

Even if I did know exactly how many people much collateral damage was damaged inside that blast radius, I am not sure it would matter. *Every job is important.* I pointed the laser.

hear piercing whistle ballistic
                              missile

.... *a t o m*
i z e d

I want to kneel and (s)weep
                              their ashes into a manila
envelope

the necessary people signed
    the documents inside.

AMERICA!
~~South, Central, North,~~ United States

Prisoners of War

_____

Detainees

Say something about the same sides of different coins:
Bodies are currency.

Object placed to be rescued or raped or to propel our progressiveness. Shut up. We let you out of the kitchen and onto the front lines.

You wear a badge or mask or bumper sticker: Military Wife. Pack your kids' lunches for school. Metallic squishiness of Capri Sun, brown saliva paste of animal crackers, crushed plastic of Lunchables. Once they are on the bus laughing you will be visited by a Casualty Notification Officer. He will regret to inform you.

White powder mountains. Diaspora through deserts. Further hollowed bellies. Half faces. All injured in the line of our duty. They cannot file a claim for disability.

My country says you did something
wrong. I will tell myself that until I feel
better. I will tell myself that until I feel
better. I will tell myself that until I feel
better. I will tell myself that until I feel
better. I will tell you that until

in the villages of Khakriz, U.S warplanes bombed the isolated village of Asmanzai for 5 nights, killing 70 innocent townspeople and leveling the Shah Agha Sufi mosque, dozens of homes, and stores. No Taliban fighters were killed. Residents said 19 people (including 11 children) were killed in the home of businessman, Shah Mohammed. The bodies of 2 children were never recovered. Shah's brother, Wali, said, "Some of them had their arms cut off, their heads cut off, we found pieces of the children, their hair, noses, bones." Villagers ran south into the desert, not daring to return almost the whole village was wiped out. Before bombing, the population was 200, but only half of them could escape the 25 bombs. The gardens of famous Kandahri pomegranate were rooted out. Thousands of animals were also killed.

"Most of the residents of this village were farmers," said Subhan Khan, a resident of the village. "I suddenly overheard the explosions. I came out from my home, and it was the decisive moment because as I stepped out a bomb hit my home destroying it and killing all my family members."

Subhan's three children, wife, and aging parents were killed in the air strikes meant to target military installations and Al-Qaeda's training camps. "On the one hand, America is dropping bombs on us and on the other hand it is dropping food packets. We will die of hunger but never accept this food," Subhan said a circle of trampled wheat stalks and dark bloodstains marked the place. Where the three villagers were killed. One of them a 13-year old boy, gunned down in an American air attack as they hid in the wheat fields. Villagers said they fled their homes in the dark as planes and helicopters strafed the houses and fields, and fired rockets. Then dozens of soldiers rappelled to search the houses.

"They were hiding when they were hit, they were crouching down," said Saleh Muhammad, who found his brother, Lal and his son, Mohibullah, 13, and a neighbor, Sher Muhammad, two days later lying in the wheat field. Another teenager, Mira Jan, a farmhand, was found dead. He was shot through the stomach while sleeping outside in the muddy front yard of the farmhouse where he worked.

Muhammad Jan, 35, ran out of his house but no one saw how he died. His brother Pir Muhammad was harvesting his poppies the next morning when neighbors called him. They had found his brother in the field. "I only saw his face," Pir Muhammad said. "There was a big hole between his eyes. You could put three fingers in the hole"

Cast

in order of disappearance

KILLED IRAQI CIVILIAN	SAHAR KHALIL
KILLED IRAQI CIVILIAN	UM AQEEL KHALIL
KILLED IRAQI CIVILIAN	HUSSEIN OSMAN
KILLED IRAQI CIVILIAN	IMRAN SREIHNIN
KILLED IRAQI CIVILIAN	AHMAD AL-BATH
KILLED IRAQI CIVILIAN	ADBULLAH ABABNEH
KILLED IRAQI CIVILIAN	SUFIAN AL-BATAYNEH
KILLED IRAQI CIVILIAN	BROTHER OF THAIR MOHE EL-DIN
KILLED IRAQI CIVILIAN	MOTHER OF ZARA
KILLED IRAQI CIVILIAN	HUSBAND OF METAQ ALI
KILLED IRAQI CIVILIAN	CHILD OF COUPLE
KILLED IRAQI CIVILIAN	KHURSA ALI
KILLED IRAQI CIVILIAN	JALAL AL-YUSSUF
KILLED IRAQI CIVILIAN	IBRAHIM AL-YUSSUF
KILLED IRAQI CIVILIAN	SAMAR HUSSEIN
KILLED IRAQI CIVILIAN	BROTHER OF HAIDER MOHAMMED
KILLED IRAQI CIVILIAN	BROTHER OF HAIDER MOHAMMED
KILLED IRAQI CIVILIAN	MADEEHA ADB KATHEM
KILLED IRAQI CIVILIAN	ALI SABAH EADAN
KILLED IRAQI CIVILIAN	MALEK SABAH EADAN
KILLED IRAQI CIVILIAN	HUSHAM SABAH EADAN
KILLED IRAQI CIVILIAN	SABAH GEDAN KARBEET
KILLED IRAQI CIVILIAN	KAMEELA ABD KATHEM
KILLED IRAQI CIVILIAN	AZHAR ALI TAHER
KILLED IRAQI CIVILIAN	ABBAS ESMAEEL ABBAS
KILLED IRAQI CIVILIAN	MUNA TAHA ABBAS
KILLED IRAQI CIVILIAN	MUHAMMED TAHA ABBAS
KILLED IRAQI CIVILIAN	ESMAEEL ABBAS HAMZA
KILLED IRAQI CIVILIAN	HEMDAN HABY HESHFAN GASHAME
KILLED IRAQI CIVILIAN	WIFE OF HAYTHAM RAHI
KILLED IRAQI CIVILIAN	PATIENT IN AMBULANCE
KILLED IRAQI CIVILIAN	COUSIN OF ALI ABED QASSEM
KILLED IRAQI CIVILIAN	SISTER OF ALI ABED QASSEM
KILLED IRAQI CIVILIAN	SISTER-IN-LAW OF ALI ABED QASSEM
KILLED IRAQI CIVILIAN	MOTHER OF ALI ABED QASSEM
KILLED IRAQI CIVILIAN	MOHAMMED JASSIM
KILLED IRAQI CIVILIAN	HUSSEIN JASSIM
KILLED IRAQI CIVILIAN	ALI JASSIM
KILLED IRAQI CIVILIAN	THAMER AIZ
KILLED IRAQI CIVILIAN	NAJAH ABDEL-RIDHA

KILLED IRAQI CIVILIAN	VALANTINA YONAS
KILLED IRAQI CIVILIAN	BROTHER OF BAKHAT HASSAN
KILLED IRAQI CIVILIAN	NIECE OF BAKHAT HASSAN
KILLED IRAQI CIVILIAN	SISTER-IN-LAW OF BAKHAT HASSAN
KILLED IRAQI CIVILIAN	BROTHER OF BAKHAT HASSAN
KILLED IRAQI CIVILIAN	MOTHER OF BAKHAT HASSAN
KILLED IRAQI CIVILIAN	FATHER OF BAKHAT HASSAN
KILLED IRAQI CIVILIAN	SON OF BAKHAT HASSAN
KILLED IRAQI CIVILIAN	DAUGHTER OF BAKHAT HASSAN
KILLED IRAQI CIVILIAN	DAUGHTER OF BAKHAT HASSAN
KILLED IRAQI CIVILIAN	WIFE OF BROTHER OF RAZAL AL-KAZEM
KILLED IRAQI CIVILIAN	BROTHER OF RAZAL AL-KAZEM
KILLED IRAQI CIVILIAN	BROTHER OF RAZAL AL-KAZEM
KILLED IRAQI CIVILIAN	WIFE OF BROTHER OF RAZAL AL-KAZEM
KILLED IRAQI CIVILIAN	MOTHER OF RAZAL AL-KAZEM
KILLED IRAQI CIVILIAN	FATHER OF RAZAL AL-KAZEM
KILLED IRAQI CIVILIAN	CHILD OF RAZAL AL-KAZEM
KILLED IRAQI CIVILIAN	CHILD OF RAZAL AL-KAZEM
KILLED IRAQI CIVILIAN	CHILD OF RAZAL AL-KAZEM
KILLED IRAQI CIVILIAN	CHILD OF RAZAL AL-KAZEM
KILLED IRAQI CIVILIAN	CHILD OF RAZAL AL-KAZEM
KILLED IRAQI CIVILIAN	CHILD OF RAZAL AL-KAZEM
KILLED IRAQI CIVILIAN	CHILD OF RAZAL AL-KAZEM
KILLED IRAQI CIVILIAN	WIFE OF RAZAL AL-KAZEM
KILLED IRAQI CIVILIAN	NORA SABAH GADAN
KILLED IRAQI CIVILIAN	FATEMA ZABOON MAKTOOF
KILLED IRAQI CIVILIAN	SABEHA AWAD MERDAS
KILLED IRAQI CIVILIAN	KHAIRIAH MAHMOUD
KILLED IRAQI CIVILIAN	IHAB ABED
KILLED IRAQI CIVILIAN	WISSAM ABED
KILLED IRAQI CIVILIAN	NOOR ELHUDA SAAD
KILLED IRAQI CIVILIAN	AMMAR MUHAMMED
KILLED IRAQI CIVILIAN	HASSAN IYAD
KILLED IRAQI CIVILIAN	ZAINAB AKRAM
KILLED IRAQI CIVILIAN	MUSTAFA AKRAM
KILLED IRAQI CIVILIAN	ZEENA AKRAM
KILLED IRAQI CIVILIAN	UNCLE OF OMAR
KILLED IRAQI CIVILIAN	SISTER OF OMAR
KILLED IRAQI CIVILIAN	SISTER OF OMAR
KILLED IRAQI CIVILIAN	BROTHER OF OMAR
KILLED IRAQI CIVILIAN	MOTHER OF OMAR
KILLED IRAQI CIVILIAN	FATHER OF OMAR
KILLED IRAQI CIVILIAN	ADBUD SARHAN
KILLED IRAQI CIVILIAN	KAVEH GOLESTAN
KILLED IRAQI CIVILIAN	WALID ABU SHAKER

KILLED IRAQI CIVILIAN	DAUGHTER OF MONA GHOLAM
KILLED IRAQI CIVILIAN	VALENTIA BASHAR FARAJ
KILLED IRAQI CIVILIAN	MAHROOSA JARJIS
KILLED IRAQI CIVILIAN	MANAL SAAD ALLAH MATTI
KILLED IRAQI CIVILIAN	HILAL FARIJ SILO
KILLED IRAQI CIVILIAN	NIECE OF BAKHAT HASSAN
KILLED IRAQI CIVILIAN	SISTER-IN-LAW OF BAKHAT HASSAN
KILLED IRAQI CIVILIAN	TARAS PROTSYUK
KILLED IRAQI CIVILIAN	UDAY AL SHIMAREY
KILLED IRAQI CIVILIAN	ARKAN MAJID
KILLED IRAQI CIVILIAN	GHASSAN MAJID
KILLED IRAQI CIVILIAN	RASHID MAJID
KILLED IRAQI CIVILIAN	CHRISTIAN LIEBIG
KILLED IRAQI CIVILIAN	JULIO ANGUITA PARRADO
KILLED IRAQI CIVILIAN	FAMILY OF SALER HAMZEH ALI MOUSSAWI
KILLED IRAQI CIVILIAN	FAMILY OF SALER HAMZEH ALI MOUSSAWI
KILLED IRAQI CIVILIAN	FAMILY OF SALER HAMZEH ALI MOUSSAWI
KILLED IRAQI CIVILIAN	FAMILY OF SALER HAMZEH ALI MOUSSAWI
KILLED IRAQI CIVILIAN	FAMILY OF SALER HAMZEH ALI MOUSSAWI
KILLED IRAQI CIVILIAN	FAMILY OF SALER HAMZEH ALI MOUSSAWI
KILLED IRAQI CIVILIAN	FAMILY OF SALER HAMZEH ALI MOUSSAWI
KILLED IRAQI CIVILIAN	FAMILY OF SALER HAMZEH ALI MOUSSAWI
KILLED IRAQI CIVILIAN	FAMILY OF SALER HAMZEH ALI MOUSSAWI
KILLED IRAQI CIVILIAN	FAMILY OF SALER HAMZEH ALI MOUSSAWI
KILLED IRAQI CIVILIAN	FAMILY OF SALER HAMZEH ALI MOUSSAWI
KILLED IRAQI CIVILIAN	BASHAR HANDI
KILLED IRAQI CIVILIAN	WADHAR HANDI
KILLED IRAQI CIVILIAN	KAMARAN ABDURAZAQ MUHAMED
KILLED IRAQI CIVILIAN	CHILD OF MAHMOUD ALI HAMADI
KILLED IRAQI CIVILIAN	CHILD OF MAHMOUD ALI HAMADI
KILLED IRAQI CIVILIAN	CHILD OF MAHMOUD ALI HAMADI
KILLED IRAQI CIVILIAN	WIFE OF MAHMOUD ALI HAMADI
KILLED IRAQI CIVILIAN	COUSIN OF TAHA KUDAIR
KILLED IRAQI CIVILIAN	BROTHER OF CHILD INJURED
KILLED IRAQI CIVILIAN	FATHER OF CHILD INJURED
KILLED IRAQI CIVILIAN	MOHAMMAD AL-BARHEINI
KILLED IRAQI CIVILIAN	BROTHER OF FAHAL ABDUL HAMID
KILLED IRAQI CIVILIAN	NIECE OF MALIK AL-KHARBIT
KILLED IRAQI CIVILIAN	SISTER OF MALIK AL-KHARBIT
KILLED IRAQI CIVILIAN	WIFE OF MALIK OF AL-KHARBIT
KILLED IRAQI CIVILIAN	MALIK AL-KHARBIT
KILLED IRAQI CIVILIAN	DUAA RAHEEM
KILLED IRAQI CIVILIAN	NORA ?, COUSIN OF HAITHEM TAMIMI
KILLED IRAQI CIVILIAN	HAITHEM TAMIMI
KILLED IRAQI CIVILIAN	MOHAMMED EL-FAYATH

KILLED IRAQI CIVILIAN	ABDUL HUSSEIN EL-FAYATH
KILLED IRAQI CIVILIAN	JUMHOUR EL-ZERGANY
KILLED IRAQI CIVILIAN	MUTHER ABADI
KILLED IRAQI CIVILIAN	ABU SALAM ABDUL GAFUR
KILLED IRAQI CIVILIAN	ALI RAMZI
KILLED IRAQI CIVILIAN	JASIM MOHAMMED OMAR
KILLED IRAQI CIVILIAN	HANSA MOHAMMAD OMAR
KILLED IRAQI CIVILIAN	VATCHE ARSLANIAN
KILLED IRAQI CIVILIAN	TAREQ AYOUB
KILLED IRAQI CIVILIAN	JOSE COUSO
KILLED IRAQI CIVILIAN	SA'ALEH AL-JUMAILI
KILLED IRAQI CIVILIAN	SALEH QUDR ABBAS FARHAN
KILLED IRAQI CIVILIAN	AIFAN HUSSEIN ULAJ
KILLED IRAQI CIVILIAN	ANIS MUHAMMED ALWANI
KILLED IRAQI CIVILIAN	MUHAMMED IMAD ABDU YASSIN
KILLED IRAQI CIVILIAN	SAMIR ALI AL-DULAIMI
KILLED IRAQI CIVILIAN	ABD AL-QADIR
KILLED IRAQI CIVILIAN	WALEED SALEH ABDEL-LATIF
KILLED IRAQI CIVILIAN	COUSIN OF SALAH ABDULLAH HAMID
KILLED IRAQI CIVILIAN	HUSSEIN RASHID
KILLED IRAQI CIVILIAN	TUAMER ABDEL HAMID
KILLED IRAQI CIVILIAN	LAMIYA ALI
KILLED IRAQI CIVILIAN	DANA ALI
KILLED IRAQI CIVILIAN	WIFE OF SON OF TAMIR KAZAL
KILLED IRAQI CIVILIAN	SON OF TAMIR KAZAL
KILLED IRAQI CIVILIAN	SON OF TAMIR KAZAL
KILLED IRAQI CIVILIAN	SON OF TAMIR KAZAL
KILLED IRAQI CIVILIAN	WIFE OF TAMIR KAZAL
KILLED IRAQI CIVILIAN	KHAZAL SABER
KILLED IRAQI CIVILIAN	FRIEND OF ALI MAHDI KATHUM
KILLED IRAQI CIVILIAN	COUSIN OF ALI MAHDI KATHUM
KILLED IRAQI CIVILIAN	MOHAMMED ALHAMDANI
KILLED IRAQI CIVILIAN	YASIREE AHMES AL-HADDI
KILLED IRAQI CIVILIAN	HAMEID HUSSEIN
KILLED IRAQI CIVILIAN	SALAM MUHAMAD RASHID
KILLED IRAQI CIVILIAN	HODEIMA HAMEED KHALAF
KILLED IRAQI CIVILIAN	MONA JASSIM KHALAF
KILLED IRAQI CIVILIAN	WA'EL RAHIM JABAR
KILLED IRAQI CIVILIAN	AHMED HAMID AL RIFAAI
KILLED IRAQI CIVILIAN	FATHER OF HADY JABER
KILLED IRAQI CIVILIAN	HADY JABER
KILLED IRAQI CIVILIAN	MUSLIM AZIZ ISSA
KILLED IRAQI CIVILIAN	RATHY NAMMA
KILLED IRAQI CIVILIAN	DAOUD QAIS
KILLED IRAQI CIVILIAN	SA'ADI SULEIMAN IRBRAHIM

KILLED IRAQI CIVILIAN	ABD AL-JABBAR MOSSA
KILLED IRAQI CIVILIAN	NADHEM ABDULLAH AL-SAQER
KILLED IRAQI CIVILIAN	FALAH DULAIMI
KILLED IRAQI CIVILIAN	KHALED LAHOUMI AHMED
KILLED IRAQI CIVILIAN	AHMED JABAR KARHEEM
KILLED IRAQI CIVILIAN	ALI SALIM
KILLED IRAQI CIVILIAN	ABID SLEWA
KILLED IRAQI CIVILIAN	COUSIN OF THA KUDAIR
KILLED IRAQI CIVILIAN	UMAR HATHARI AL UQAILI
KILLED IRAQI CIVILIAN	MUHAMMAD IMAD ABBUD
KILLED IRAQI CIVILIAN	GHANAM AL-JUMAILI
KILLED IRAQI CIVILIAN	SAME HALOUM
KILLED IRAQI CIVILIAN	ABDUL HALIM HALOUM
KILLED IRAQI CIVILIAN	ABDEL-SALAM AL-SAMEEN
KILLED IRAQI CIVILIAN	MAHA KHALIL
KILLED IRAQI CIVILIAN	HAKIMA KHALIL
KILLED IRAQI CIVILIAN	JUMAA ABU ZAATIR
KILLED IRAQI CIVILIAN	MR. MATTAR
KILLED IRAQI CIVILIAN	TAREQ MOHAMMED
KILLED IRAQI CIVILIAN	JA'FAR MUSA HASHEM
KILLED IRAQI CIVILIAN	HASSAN HEKMET
KILLED IRAQI CIVILIAN	ALAA JASSEM
KILLED IRAQI CIVILIAN	DILAR DABABA
KILLED IRAQI CIVILIAN	AKEL ABEDAD HUSSAIN JABAR
KILLED IRAQI CIVILIAN	QASSIM ZUBAR
KILLED IRAQI CIVILIAN	AMIR ALI JASSIM
KILLED IRAQI CIVILIAN	ABD ALI JASSIM
KILLED IRAQI CIVILIAN	HAMZA ALI JASSIM
KILLED IRAQI CIVILIAN	ALI JASSIM
KILLED IRAQI CIVILIAN	JASEEM AK-JUBARI
KILLED IRAQI CIVILIAN	MAHDI AL-JUBARI
KILLED IRAQI CIVILIAN	JASSIM RUMAID MOHAMMED
KILLED IRAQI CIVILIAN	HASHIM MOHAMMED AHNI
KILLED IRAQI CIVILIAN	MEHMID MUTLAG
KILLED IRAQI CIVILIAN	NAGEM SADOON HATAB
KILLED IRAQI CIVILIAN	MR. HAMZA
KILLED IRAQI CIVILIAN	ANAS BASIL HAMED
KILLED IRAQI CIVILIAN	OMAR AL-NAJJAR
KILLED IRAQI CIVILIAN	ALI GHAZI
KILLED IRAQI CIVILIAN	AHMED AL-JURAYFI
KILLED IRAQI CIVILIAN	UDAY AHMED
KILLED IRAQI CIVILIAN	ABDULLAH MAHMUD AL-AMIN
KILLED IRAQI CIVILIAN	RICHARD WILD
KILLED IRAQI CIVILIAN	AHMAD KARIM
KILLED IRAQI CIVILIAN	SON OF SHAAKER MAHMOUD MOKLEF

KILLED IRAQI CIVILIAN	SHAAKER MAHMOUD MOKLEF
KILLED IRAQI CIVILIAN	WIFE OF SHAAKER MAHOUD MOKLEF
KILLED IRAQI CIVILIAN	BROTHER OF ADBUL RAHMAN ABDUL KAREEM
KILLED IRAQI CIVILIAN	LAITH KHALIL
KILLED IRAQI CIVILIAN	JEREMY LITTLE
KILLED IRAQI CIVILIAN	QAHTAN HASHEN
KILLED IRAQI CIVILIAN	ABDULLAH MAHMUD AL-KHATTAB
KILLED IRAQI CIVILIAN	MAZEN ANTOINE HANNA NORADDIN
KILLED IRAQI CIVILIAN	MUHANNAD ?
KILLED IRAQI CIVILIAN	MUHAMMAD SUBHI HASSAN AL-QUBAISI
KILLED IRAQI CIVILIAN	COUSIN OF WASAMA AL-SALAH
KILLED IRAQI CIVILIAN	HAIFA AZIZ DAOUD
KILLED IRAQI CIVILIAN	SADIA ABDULLAH HUSSAIN
KILLED IRAQI CIVILIAN	GHAZI MUSA HASSAN
KILLED IRAQI CIVILIAN	TASSIR ABDUL WAHED
KILLED IRAQI CIVILIAN	MIRVET ADIL ABD AL-KARIM AL-KAWWAZ
KILLED IRAQI CIVILIAN	OLAA ADIL ABD AL-KARIM AL-KAWWAZ
KILLED IRAQI CIVILIAN	ADEL ABD AL-KARIM AL-KAWWAZ
KILLED IRAQI CIVILIAN	ABED ABD AL-KARIM HASSAN
KILLED IRAQI CIVILIAN	HAZIM JUMAH KATI
KILLED IRAQI CIVILIAN	HASSAN ABBAD SAID
KILLED IRAQI CIVILIAN	HAMAD ANTAR SHANDUKH
KILLED IRAQI CIVILIAN	AHSAN BARDAN AFLOK
KILLED IRAQI CIVILIAN	YAHYA BARDAN AFLOK
KILLED IRAQI CIVILIAN	KHUDHAYR ABBAS JASIM
KILLED IRAQI CIVILIAN	COUSIN OF TALEB ISSA
KILLED IRAQI CIVILIAN	AHMED HAIDER
KILLED IRAQI CIVILIAN	SALIM HUSSEIN
KILLED IRAQI CIVILIAN	BROTHER OF MOHAMMED HAMID
KILLED IRAQI CIVILIAN	AHMED ?
KILLED IRAQI CIVILIAN	SHA'LAN MUNIF AL-FAYSAL
KILLED IRAQI CIVILIAN	KAMEELA MAHOOD RIDHA
KILLED IRAQI CIVILIAN	EZHAR MAHMOOD RIDHA
KILLED IRAQI CIVILIAN	DR. MOHAMMED AL-RAWI
KILLED IRAQI CIVILIAN	MUSHRAK AL-IBRAHIM
KILLED IRAQI CIVILIAN	MAZEN ELAYAS ALBERT
KILLED IRAQI CIVILIAN	HAIDER AL-SHIHLAWI
KILLED IRAQI CIVILIAN	NADISHA YASASSRI RANMUTHU
KILLED IRAQI CIVILIAN	MUSTAFA HUSSEIN
KILLED IRAQI CIVILIAN	OMAR KAHTAN MOHAMED AL-ORFALI
KILLED IRAQI CIVILIAN	SAAD HERMIZ ABONA
KILLED IRAQI CIVILIAN	NADIA YOUNES
KILLED IRAQI CIVILIAN	FIONA WATSON
KILLED IRAQI CIVILIAN	BASIM MAHMOOD UTAIWI
KILLED IRAQI CIVILIAN	MARTHA TEAS

KILLED IRAQI CIVILIAN	CHRISTOPHER KLEIN-BEEKMAN
KILLED IRAQI CIVILIAN	JEAN-SELIM KANAAN
KILLED IRAQI CIVILIAN	IHSSAN TAHA HUSAIN
KILLED IRAQI CIVILIAN	REZA HOSSEINI
KILLED IRAQI CIVILIAN	RICHARD HOOPER
KILLED IRAQI CIVILIAN	RANILO BUENAVENTURA
KILLED IRAQI CIVILIAN	LEEN ASSAD AL-QUADI
KILLED IRAQI CIVILIAN	RAID SHAKER MUSTAFA AL-MAHDAWI
KILLED IRAQI CIVILIAN	EMAAD AHMED SLAMAN AL-JOBORY
KILLED IRAQI CIVILIAN	REHAM AL-FARRA
KILLED IRAQI CIVILIAN	SERGIO VIEIRA DE MELLO
KILLED IRAQI CIVILIAN	MAZEN DANA
KILLED IRAQI CIVILIAN	FARID ABDUL KHAHIR
KILLED IRAQI CIVILIAN	ALI MUSHIN
KILLED IRAQI CIVILIAN	HASSAN HAMEED NASIR
KILLED IRAQI CIVILIAN	ALAA ALI SALEH
KILLED IRAQI CIVILIAN	MOHAMMED HILAL NAHI
KILLED IRAQI CIVILIAN	ALI SALMAN
KILLED IRAQI CIVILIAN	SAYF ALI
KILLED IRAQI CIVILIAN	OBEED HETHERE RADAD
KILLED IRAQI CIVILIAN	SON OF LOCAL SUNNI CHIEF
KILLED IRAQI CIVILIAN	SON OF LOCAL SUNNI CHIEF
KILLED IRAQI CIVILIAN	HASSAN MAHMOUD ABBAS
KILLED IRAQI CIVILIAN	AFRAH ABDUL MONEEM
KILLED IRAQI CIVILIAN	MAKKI HASSAN TAWIYEH
KILLED IRAQI CIVILIAN	FALAH MOHAMMAD AJILI
KILLED IRAQI CIVILIAN	IAN RIMELL
KILLED IRAQI CIVILIAN	OMAR SAAD JASSEM
KILLED IRAQI CIVILIAN	JASSEM JUBARA
KILLED IRAQI CIVILIAN	TAHA HAMDED KHAFI
KILLED IRAQI CIVILIAN	ABD-AL-RAZZAQ AL-HASHIMI
KILLED IRAQI CIVILIAN	MARDAN MUHAMMAD HASSAN
KILLED IRAQI CIVILIAN	FARAH FAHDIL
KILLED IRAQI CIVILIAN	HAMA HUSSEIN
KILLED IRAQI CIVILIAN	MOHAMMED BAQUIR AL-HAKIM
KILLED IRAQI CIVILIAN	WALID FAYAY MAZBAN
KILLED IRAQI CIVILIAN	TARIQ MOHAMMED ZAID
KILLED IRAQI CIVILIAN	HANAN SALEF MALTRUD
KILLED IRAQI CIVILIAN	NADAN YONADAM
KILLED IRAQI CIVILIAN	ALYA AHMAD SOUSA
KILLED IRAQI CIVILIAN	KHIDIR SALEEM SAHIR
KILLED IRAQI CIVILIAN	MANUEL MARTIN-OAR FERNANDEZ-HEREDIA
KILLED IRAQI CIVILIAN	ARTHUR HELTON
KILLED IRAQI CIVILIAN	GILLAN CLARK
KILLED IRAQI CIVILIAN	MOTHER OF BOY KILLED

KILLED IRAQI CIVILIAN	JABBAR ALI MOHAMMED
KILLED IRAQI CIVILIAN	KHALIL JADDUH AL-JULEIMI
KILLED IRAQI CIVILIAN	BEIJAH AL JULEIMI
KILLED IRAQI CIVILIAN	AMAL AL-JULEIMI
KILLED IRAQI CIVILIAN	DUREID HASSAN ALWAN
KILLED IRAQI CIVILIAN	WUAISE JABER
KILLED IRAQI CIVILIAN	ADEL ISMAIL
KILLED IRAQI CIVILIAN	MAZEN SHOUKR
KILLED IRAQI CIVILIAN	NASR-AL-DIN QASIM
KILLED IRAQI CIVILIAN	SALEM KHALIL JUMAILI
KILLED IRAQI CIVILIAN	SAADI FAYAD JUMAILI
KILLED IRAQI CIVILIAN	ALI KHALAF JUMAILI
KILLED IRAQI CIVILIAN	SALAM MOHAMMED
KILLED IRAQI CIVILIAN	DR. ABDULLAH AL-FADHIL
KILLED IRAQI CIVILIAN	AQUILA AL-HASHIMI
KILLED IRAQI CIVILIAN	SAAD MOHAMMED SULTAN
KILLED IRAQI CIVILIAN	BAHA SALIM MUSA
KILLED IRAQI CIVILIAN	SUFYAN DAOUD AL-KUBAISI
KILLED IRAQI CIVILIAN	KHEDEIR MEKHALEF ALI
KILLED IRAQI CIVILIAN	SAMI HASSAN SAREF
KILLED IRAQI CIVILIAN	HASSAN ALI AHMAD
KILLED IRAQI CIVILIAN	YOUNES MOHAMMAD-YARI
KILLED IRAQI CIVILIAN	SUBHI SATTAM GUOOD
KILLED IRAQI CIVILIAN	PERSONAL DRIVER OF BUSINESSMAN
KILLED IRAQI CIVILIAN	SECRETARY OF BUSINESSMAN
KILLED IRAQI CIVILIAN	ALAA ABDEL KADER
KILLED IRAQI CIVILIAN	JIHAN OMRAN
KILLED IRAQI CIVILIAN	HAIDAR AL-BAAJ
KILLED IRAQI CIVILIAN	ABU ZANAIB
KILLED IRAQI CIVILIAN	RUF'IL SILAYWAH
KILLED IRAQI CIVILIAN	DHIYAH KHALAF
KILLED IRAQI CIVILIAN	FAROOQ ATI LASAM AL-ZUHAIRI
KILLED IRAQI CIVILIAN	WIFE OF ABD-AL-QADIR ABD-AL-RAHMAN
KILLED IRAQI CIVILIAN	ABD-AL-QADIR ABD-AL-RAHMAN
KILLED IRAQI CIVILIAN	MOHAMMAD GHAFUR
KILLED IRAQI CIVILIAN	QAHTAN MOHAMMAD OLAYAN
KILLED IRAQI CIVILIAN	KHALIL KARAM HASNAWI
KILLED IRAQI CIVILIAN	SAFA SABAH LORA
KILLED IRAQI CIVILIAN	RAED KAMEL MAHDI
KILLED IRAQI CIVILIAN	AHMED ABDEL AL-SATTAR
KILLED IRAQI CIVILIAN	NAMARA SALEH
KILLED IRAQI CIVILIAN	WILLAM KAISER NAPOLEON
KILLED IRAQI CIVILIAN	DANNY ISSAC
KILLED IRAQI CIVILIAN	AHMAD SULAYMAN
KILLED IRAQI CIVILIAN	MARDAN ALI HAMAD

KILLED IRAQI CIVILIAN	AKRAM SULAYMAN
KILLED IRAQI CIVILIAN	HUSAYN DAHKIL AHMAD
KILLED IRAQI CIVILIAN	DEKRAN GREGOR
KILLED IRAQI CIVILIAN	ZOHEIR ABDALLAH AHMAD AL-SHEIKHLY
KILLED IRAQI CIVILIAN	OMAR AHMED
KILLED IRAQI CIVILIAN	DAUTHER OF SHAMAR
KILLED IRAQI CIVILIAN	DONIYA ABBAS
KILLED IRAQI CIVILIAN	SHAMAR ABBAS
KILLED IRAQI CIVILIAN	MOHAMMED MIZEL HASAN
KILLED IRAQI CIVILIAN	MUHSEN ABDUL WAHID AL-HAJAMA
KILLED IRAQI CIVILIAN	TAYSEER ?
KILLED IRAQI CIVILIAN	WALEED KHUDAYER
KILLED IRAQI CIVILIAN	AHMED KHUDAYER
KILLED IRAQI CIVILIAN	FARIS ABDUL RAZZAQ ASSAM
KILLED IRAQI CIVILIAN	AYAT JAWRANI
KILLED IRAQI CIVILIAN	MUHAMMAD JAWRANI
KILLED IRAQI CIVILIAN	HAMID HAADI AL-AY'BI
KILLED IRAQI CIVILIAN	SAFAR RADI ZBOON
KILLED IRAQI CIVILIAN	THAMIR AL-FILAHI
KILLED IRAQI CIVILIAN	ISAM AL-DARUBI
KILLED IRAQI CIVILIAN	KARIM AL-HANSHAWI
KILLED IRAQI CIVILIAN	MUHAMMAD AL-SAB-AWI
KILLED IRAQI CIVILIAN	DR. ISAM SHARIF AL-TIKRITI
KILLED IRAQI CIVILIAN	NAZEM BAJI
KILLED IRAQI CIVILIAN	MARWAN HAYAD AL-ISSAWI
KILLED IRAQI CIVILIAN	SAMI SALIH AHMAD
KILLED IRAQI CIVILIAN	AMAAR FARMAN
KILLED IRAQI CIVILIAN	ALI MOHAMMED ZIBARI
KILLED IRAQI CIVILIAN	HANAN SHMAILAWI
KILLED IRAQI CIVILIAN	MOHANNAD GHAZI AL KAABI
KILLED IRAQI CIVILIAN	WIFE OF YUNES IBRAHIM HATEM
KILLED IRAQI CIVILIAN	MOHAMMED ABDUL RIDHA SALIM
KILLED IRAQI CIVILIAN	OSMAN PELTEK
KILLED IRAQI CIVILIAN	LAITH ALI TOMEH
KILLED IRAQI CIVILIAN	ISMAIL YUSSEF SADDEK
KILLED IRAQI CIVILIAN	MUNADEL AL-JUMEILI
KILLED IRAQI CIVILIAN	HUSSEIN AHMED SHEHAB
KILLED IRAQI CIVILIAN	MOHAN JABER AL-SHOUEILI
KILLED IRAQI CIVILIAN	COUSINS OF ARKAN YASS
KILLED IRAQI CIVILIAN	DAOUD YASS
KILLED IRAQI CIVILIAN	SALMAN YASS
KILLED IRAQI CIVILIAN	AIDAN EZZEDIN
KILLED IRAQI CIVILIAN	MUSTAFA ZAIDAN AL-KHALEEFA
KILLED IRAQI CIVILIAN	ASAAD AL-SHAREEDA
KILLED IRAQI CIVILIAN	SAMI SHAKIR AL-SAFAR

KILLED IRAQI CIVILIAN	ZIAD YASS ABBAS
KILLED IRAQI CIVILIAN	SHAKER HEKMAT
KILLED IRAQI CIVILIAN	BASSIM ?
KILLED IRAQI CIVILIAN	MUHAMMAD ABDUL NABI AL-GISHI
KILLED IRAQI CIVILIAN	AHMED SHAWKAT
KILLED IRAQI CIVILIAN	DAWOOD MAZIN THAWIN
KILLED IRAQI CIVILIAN	HUSSEIN KAMEL HADI DAWOOD ZUBEIDI
KILLED IRAQI CIVILIAN	ABDEL SALAM QANBAR
KILLED IRAQI CIVILIAN	ALI KARIM ABBAS
KILLED IRAQI CIVILIAN	IBITHAL ABDUL-RIHMAN
KILLED IRAQI CIVILIAN	ALI KHALEEL
KILLED IRAQI CIVILIAN	ABBAS GHAIDAN
KILLED IRAQI CIVILIAN	MOHAMMED SABAH ODAI
KILLED IRAQI CIVILIAN	SABAH ODAI
KILLED IRAQI CIVILIAN	IBRAHIM ODAI
KILLED IRAQI CIVILIAN	MOHAMMED ALWANI
KILLED IRAQI CIVILIAN	NOZAD AHMED
KILLED IRAQI CIVILIAN	MASSIR ALI HUSSEIN MARZEH
KILLED IRAQI CIVILIAN	COUSIN OF SHEIKH AMER
KILLED IRAQI CIVILIAN	SARGOUN NANOU MURADO
KILLED IRAQI CIVILIAN	AKIL HUSSAIN NAIM
KILLED IRAQI CIVILIAN	HUSSEIN ALI
KILLED IRAQI CIVILIAN	HAMUD KAZEM AL-MUHMADAWI
KILLED IRAQI CIVILIAN	PETER VARGA-BALAZS
KILLED IRAQI CIVILIAN	SON OF KHALID VICTOR
KILLED IRAQI CIVILIAN	KHALID VICTOR
KILLED IRAQI CIVILIAN	HUSSEIN WAHID
KILLED IRAQI CIVILIAN	WAHID AL-JUMAIDY
KILLED IRAQI CIVILIAN	MAJEED AL-JUMAIDY
KILLED IRAQI CIVILIAN	KHALID MAJEED AL-JUMAIDY
KILLED IRAQI CIVILIAN	UTHMAN AL-NUAIMAN
KILLED IRAQI CIVILIAN	WALID SALEH KASSAR
KILLED IRAQI CIVILIAN	AKRAM HANOUSH YAAQOUB
KILLED IRAQI CIVILIAN	ABDULREDA LAFTA ABDUL KAREEM
KILLED IRAQI CIVILIAN	FALLAH KHADDURI
KILLED IRAQI CIVILIAN	ABD-HUMUD MUHAWISH
KILLED IRAQI CIVILIAN	KHALAF ALUSSI
KILLED IRAQI CIVILIAN	OMAR SALEH
KILLED IRAQI CIVILIAN	SHEIK ABDEL RAZZAQ AL-LAMI
KILLED IRAQI CIVILIAN	AMIRA MAHDI SALEH
KILLED IRAQI CIVILIAN	HOSASM SHAKIR AL-DOURI
KILLED IRAQI CIVILIAN	ABDULLAH AMIN AL-KURDI
KILLED IRAQI CIVILIAN	HAMID ALI
KILLED IRAQI CIVILIAN	FATHOLLAH HEJAZI
KILLED IRAQI CIVILIAN	KATSUHIKO OKU

KILLED IRAQI CIVILIAN	MASAMOR INOUE
KILLED IRAQI CIVILIAN	JERJEES SULAIMAN ZURA
KILLED IRAQI CIVILIAN	RIAD KHALAS ABD ALLAH
KILLED IRAQI CIVILIAN	ABED HAMED MOWHOUSH
KILLED IRAQI CIVILIAN	CHILD OF RABAH HASSAN
KILLED IRAQI CIVILIAN	COUSIN OF RABAH HASSAN
KILLED IRAQI CIVILIAN	CHILD OF RABAH HASSAN
KILLED IRAQI CIVILIAN	RAED SHAALAN
KILLED IRAQI CIVILIAN	MADOOR HUSSEIN SAYER
KILLED IRAQI CIVILIAN	JUSAYA ALI SALMAN
KILLED IRAQI CIVILIAN	WIFE OF IBRAHIM ALAWI AHMAD
KILLED IRAQI CIVILIAN	ZAIDOUN FADEL HASSOUN
KILLED IRAQI CIVILIAN	MUHAMMAD
KILLED PAKISTANI CIVILIAN	ZAMAN WAZIR
KILLED PAKISTANI CIVILIAN	IRFAN WAZIR
KILLED PAKISTANI CIVILIAN	NOOR AZIZ
KILLED PAKISTANI CIVILIAN	ABDUL WASIT
KILLED PAKISTANI CIVILIAN	MOHAMMD TAHIR
KILLED PAKISTANI CIVILIAN	MAULVI KHALEEFA
KILLED PAKISTANI CIVILIAN	AZIZUL WAHAB
KILLED PAKISTANI CIVILIAN	FAZAL WAHAB
KILLED PAKISTANI CIVILIAN	ZIAUDDIN
KILLED PAKISTANI CIVILIAN	MOHAMMAD YUNUS
KILLED PAKISTANI CIVILIAN	FAZAL HAKIM
KILLED PAKISTANI CIVILIAN	ILYAS
KILLED PAKISTANI CIVILIAN	SOHAIL
KILLED PAKISTANI CIVILIAN	ASADULLAH
KILLED PAKISTANI CIVILIAN	SHOAIB
KILLED PAKISTANI CIVILIAN	KHALILULLAH
KILLED PAKISTANI CIVILIAN	NOOR MOHAMMAD
KILLED PAKISTANI CIVILIAN	KHALID
KILLED PAKISTANI CIVILIAN	SAIFULLAH
KILLED PAKISTANI CIVILIAN	RAZI MOHAMMAD
KILLED PAKISTANI CIVILIAN	MASHOOQ JAN
KILLED PAKISTANI CIVILIAN	NAWAB
KILLED PAKISTANI CIVILIAN	SULTANAT KHAN
KILLED PAKISTANI CIVILIAN	ZIAUR RAHMAN
KILLED PAKISTANI CIVILIAN	MOHAMMAD YAAS KHAN
KILLED PAKISTANI CIVILIAN	QARI ALMZEB
KILLED PAKISTANI CIVILIAN	GHULAM NABI
KILLED PAKISTANI CIVILIAN	ZIAUR RAHMAN
KILLED PAKISTANI CIVILIAN	ABDULLAH
KILLED PAKISTANI CIVILIAN	IKRAMULLAH
KILLED PAKISTANI CIVILIAN	INAUATUR RAHMAN
KILLED PAKISTANI CIVILIAN	SHAHAB UDDIN

KILLED PAKISTANI CIVILIAN	YAHYA KHAN
KILLED PAKISTANI CIVILIAN	RAHATULLAH
KILLED PAKISTANI CIVILIAN	KHAN
KILLED PAKISTANI CIVILIAN	MOHAMMAD SALIM
KILLED PAKISTANI CIVILIAN	SHAHJEHAN
KILLED PAKISTANI CIVILIAN	GUL SHER KHAN
KILLED PAKISTANI CIVILIAN	BAHKT MUNEER
KILLED PAKISTANI CIVILIAN	NUMAIR
KILLED PAKISTANI CIVILIAN	MASHOOQ KHAN
KILLED PAKISTANI CIVILIAN	IHSANULLAH
KILLED PAKISTANI CIVILIAN	LUQMAN
KILLED PAKISTANI CIVILIAN	JANNATULLAH
KILLED PAKISTANI CIVILIAN	ISMAIL
KILLED PAKISTANI CIVILIAN	TASEEL KHAN
KILLED PAKISTANI CIVILIAN	ZAHEER UDDIN
KILLED PAKISTANI CIVILIAN	QARI ISHAQ
KILLED PAKISTANI CIVILIAN	JAMSHED KHAN
KILLED PAKISTANI CIVILIAN	ALAM NABI
KILLED PAKISTANI CIVILIAN	QARI ABDUL KARIM
KILLED PAKISTANI CIVILIAN	RAHMATULLAH
KILLED PAKISTANI CIVILIAN	ABDUS SAMAD
KILLED PAKISTANI CIVILIAN	SIRAJ
KILLED PAKISTANI CIVILIAN	SAEEDULLAH
KILLED PAKISTANI CIVILIAN	ABDUL WARIS
KILLED PAKISTANI CIVILIAN	DARVESH
KILLED PAKISTANI CIVILIAN	AMER SAID
KILLED PAKISTANI CIVILIAN	SHAUKAT
KILLED PAKISTANI CIVILIAN	INAYTUR RAHMAN
KILLED PAKISTANI CIVILIAN	SALMAN
KILLED PAKISTANI CIVILIAN	FAZAL WAHAB
KILLED PAKISTANI CIVILIAN	BAACHA RAHMAN
KILLED PAKISTANI CIVILIAN	WALI-UR-RAHMAN
KILLED PAKISTANI CIVILIAN	IFTIKHAR
KILLED PAKISTANI CIVILIAN	INAYATULLAH
KILLED PAKISTANI CIVILIAN	ADNAN
KILLED PAKISTANI CIVILIAN	NAJIBULLAH
KILLED PAKISTANI CIVILIAN	NAEEMULLAH
KILLED PAKISTANI CIVILIAN	HIZBULLAH
KILLED PAKISTANI CIVILIAN	KITAB GUL
KILLED PAKISTANI CIVILIAN	WILAYAT KHAN
KILLED PAKISTANI CIVILIAN	ZABIHULLAH
KILLED PAKISTANI CIVILIAN	SHEHZAD GUL
KILLED PAKISTANI CIVILIAN	SHABIR
KILLED PAKISTANI CIVILIAN	QARI SHARIFULLAH
KILLED PAKISTANI CIVILIAN	SHAFIULLAH

KILLED PAKISTANI CIVILIAN	NAIMATULLAH
KILLED PAKISTANI CIVILIAN	SHAKIRULLAH
KILLED PAKISTANI CIVILIAN	TALHA
KILLED PAKISTANI CIVILIAN	JAMROZ KHAN
KILLED PAKISTANI CIVILIAN	TAJ ALAM
KILLED PAKISTANI CIVILIAN	KATOOR KHAN
KILLED PAKISTANI CIVILIAN	ZAHIDULLAH
KILLED PAKISTANI CIVILIAN	ABDUL GHAFOOR
KILLED PAKISTANI CIVILIAN	JAN MOHAMMAD MEHSUD
KILLED PAKISTANI CIVILIAN	DILAWAR
KILLED PAKISTANI CIVILIAN	BAKHAN
KILLED PAKISTANI CIVILIAN	NOORULLAH JAN
KILLED PAKISTANI CIVILIAN	ILYAS
KILLED PAKISTANI CIVILIAN	JAMIL
KILLED PAKISTANI CIVILIAN	FARMAN
KILLED PAKISTANI CIVILIAN	IMRAN
KILLED PAKISTANI CIVILIAN	LATIF
KILLED PAKISTANI CIVILIAN	SARDAR
KILLED PAKISTANI CIVILIAN	NAJID
KILLED PAKISTANI CIVILIAN	KAMRAN
KILLED PAKISTANI CIVILIAN	SIDDIQ
KILLED PAKISTANI CIVILIAN	NOORUL HAQ
KILLED PAKISTANI CIVILIAN	ZAMARYALAI KHAN
KILLED PAKISTANI CIVILIAN	MUHAMMAD
KILLED PAKISTANI CIVILIAN	SULTAN JAN
KILLED PAKISTANI CIVILIAN	BUKHTOOR GUL
KILLED PAKISTANI CIVILIAN	AMAN ULLAH JAN
KILLED PAKISTANI CIVILIAN	IMRAN KHAN
KILLED PAKISTANI CIVILIAN	EIDA JAN
KILLED PAKISTANI CIVILIAN	SHAKUM
KILLED PAKISTANI CIVILIAN	NASRULLAH
KILLED PAKISTANI CIVILIAN	UMAR
KILLED PAKISTANI CIVILIAN	NAEEM
KILLED PAKISTANI CIVILIAN	DIL NAWAZ
KILLED PAKISTANI CIVILIAN	YOUSAF
KILLED PAKISTANI CIVILIAN	ASHRAF
KILLED PAKISTANI CIVILIAN	NAIMATULLAH
KILLED PAKISTANI CIVILIAN	TAJ MOHAMMAD
KILLED PAKISTANI CIVILIAN	MUSA
KILLED PAKISTANI CIVILIAN	MOHAMMAD KHALEEL
KILLED PAKISTANI CIVILIAN	AZAZ-UR-REHMAN
KILLED PAKISTANI CIVILIAN	MANSOOR-UR-REHMAN
KILLED PAKISTANI CIVILIAN	KUSHDIL KHAN
KILLED PAKISTANI CIVILIAN	UBAID ULLAH
KILLED PAKISTANI CIVILIAN	RAFIQ ULLAH

KILLED PAKISTANI CIVILIAN	SAFAT ULLAH
KILLED PAKISTANI CIVILIAN	SHAMS
KILLED PAKISTANI CIVILIAN	NOOR
KILLED PAKISTANI CIVILIAN	MAJID
KILLED PAKISTANI CIVILIAN	SIRAJ
KILLED PAKISTANI CIVILIAN	MALIK GULISTAN KHAN
KILLED PAKISTANI CIVILIAN	NOOR SYED
KILLED PAKISTANI CIVILIAN	MASAL
KILLED PAKISTANI CIVILIAN	MEHBOOB
KILLED PAKISTANI CIVILIAN	WARIS
KILLED PAKISTANI CIVILIAN	WASIM
KILLED PAKISTANI CIVILIAN	IHSAN
KILLED PAKISTANI CIVILIAN	JAVED
KILLED PAKISTANI CIVILIAN	TAHIR
KILLED PAKISTANI CIVILIAN	MUNAWA
KILLED PAKISTANI CIVILIAN	ABDULLAH
KILLED PAKISTANI CIVILIAN	ABDUL LATIF
KILLED PAKISTANI CIVILIAN	MOHAMMAD SHOAIB
KILLED PAKISTANI CIVILIAN	MOHAMMAD HUSSAIN
KILLED PAKISTANI CIVILIAN	SHAFIQ
KILLED PAKISTANI CIVILIAN	QADIR
KILLED PAKISTANI CIVILIAN	SABIR
KILLED PAKISTANI CIVILIAN	IKRAM
KILLED PAKISTANI CIVILIAN	MOHIB
KILLED PAKISTANI CIVILIAN	ZAHID
KILLED PAKISTANI CIVILIAN	MASHAL
KILLED PAKISTANI CIVILIAN	SYED NOOR
KILLED PAKISTANI CIVILIAN	JEHANZEB
KILLED PAKISTANI CIVILIAN	LIAQAT
KILLED PAKISTANI CIVILIAN	DARAZ
KILLED PAKISTANI CIVILIAN	SABIL
KILLED PAKISTANI CIVILIAN	MULVI IKRAMUDDIN
KILLED PAKISTANI CIVILIAN	SYED WALI SHAH
KILLED PAKISTANI CIVILIAN	GUL DAR
KILLED PAKISTANI CIVILIAN	HAJI MUNAWAR
KILLED PAKISTANI CIVILIAN	ZAINULLAH
KILLED PAKISTANI CIVILIAN	SAHIBULLAH
KILLED PAKISTANI CIVILIAN	NAEEMULLAH
KILLED PAKISTANI CIVILIAN	FAIZULLAH
KILLED PAKISTANI CIVILIAN	RAHIMA
KILLED PAKISTANI CIVILIAN	SHAISTA
KILLED PAKISTANI CIVILIAN	MAUTULLAH JAN
KILLED PAKISTANI CIVILIAN	SABIR-UD-DIN
KILLED PAKISTANI CIVILIAN	KADANULLAH JAN
KILLED PAKISTANI CIVILIAN	ISMAIL KHAN

KILLED PAKISTANI CIVILIAN	RAZM KHAN
KILLED PAKISTANI CIVILIAN	SAKEENULLAH
KILLED PAKISTANI CIVILIAN	SHAFIQ
KILLED PAKISTANI CIVILIAN	BASHIRULLAH
KILLED PAKISTANI CIVILIAN	AMIR KHAN
KILLED PAKISTANI CIVILIAN	SHAIRULLAH
KILLED PAKISTANI CIVILIAN	ABIDULLAH
KILLED PAKISTANI CIVILIAN	FAZLE RABBI
KILLED PAKISTANI CIVILIAN	SYED NOOR
KILLED PAKISTANI CIVILIAN	SHAKIRULLAH
KILLED PAKISTANI CIVILIAN	BANARAS
KILLED PAKISTANI CIVILIAN	FAYYAZ
KILLED PAKISTANI CIVILIAN	ZAHINULLAH KHAN
KILLED PAKISTANI CIVILIAN	ASIF IQBAL
KILLED PAKISTANI CIVILIAN	KHALIQ DAD
KILLED PAKISTANI CIVILIAN	SADIQ NOOR
KILLED PAKISTANI CIVILIAN	WAJID NOOR
KILLED PAKISTANI CIVILIAN	KHALID
KILLED PAKISTANI CIVILIAN	MATIULLAH
KILLED PAKISTANI CIVILIAN	KASHIF
KILLED PAKISTANI CIVILIAN	ZAMAN
KILLED PAKISTANI CIVILIAN	WAQAR
KILLED PAKISTANI CIVILIAN	AKBAR ZAMAN
KILLED PAKISTANI CIVILIAN	MIR QALAM
KILLED PAKISTANI CIVILIAN	SAAD WALI KHAN
KILLED PAKISTANI CIVILIAN	MUHAMMAD FAYYAZ
KILLED PAKISTANI CIVILIAN	AYEESHA
KILLED PAKISTANI CIVILIAN	NOOR JANAN
KILLED PAKISTANI CIVILIAN	FARHAD
KILLED PAKISTANI CIVILIAN	SAMAD
KILLED PAKISTANI CIVILIAN	SALAM
KILLED PAKISTANI CIVILIAN	BASEER
KILLED PAKISTANI CIVILIAN	NAILA
KILLED PAKISTANI CIVILIAN	GULZAR
KILLED PAKISTANI CIVILIAN	SHAMIM
KILLED PAKISTANI CIVILIAN	MAJAN
KILLED PAKISTANI CIVILIAN	SARWAR
KILLED PAKISTANI CIVILIAN	UMM AL SHAYA
KILLED PAKISTANI CIVILIAN	HAFSAH
KILLED PAKISTANI CIVILIAN	FATIMA
KILLED PAKISTANI CIVILIAN	NISAR WAZIR
KILLED PAKISTANI CIVILIAN	NAEEM KHAN
KILLED PAKISTANI CIVILIAN	SAEED KAMAL
KILLED PAKISTANI CIVILIAN	SYED AMANULLAH
KILLED PAKISTANI CIVILIAN	SAHIB REHMAN

KILLED PAKISTANI CIVILIAN	SAKHI REHMAN
KILLED PAKISTANI CIVILIAN	SOHRAB KHAN
KILLED PAKISTANI CIVILIAN	BISMULLAH
KILLED PAKISTANI CIVILIAN	KHEMAT KHAN
KILLED PAKISTANI CIVILIAN	SAID KHAN
KILLED PAKISTANI CIVILIAN	NAMMATULLAH
KILLED PAKISTANI CIVILIAN	YAHYA
KILLED PAKISTANI CIVILIAN	SAMIN
KILLED PAKISTANI CIVILIAN	NIAMATULLAH
KILLED PAKISTANI CIVILIAN	SHAHZAD
KILLED PAKISTANI CIVILIAN	ILYAS
KILLED PAKISTANI CIVILIAN	BASHIR
KILLED PAKISTANI CIVILIAN	WAJID
KILLED PAKISTANI CIVILIAN	LAIQ
KILLED PAKISTANI CIVILIAN	NAEEM ULLAH
KILLED PAKISTANI CIVILIAN	SABIR
KILLED PAKISTANI CIVILIAN	RJAZ
KILLED PAKISTANI CIVILIAN	SHAUKATULLAH
KILLED PAKISTANI CIVILIAN	HARIS
KILLED PAKISTANI CIVILIAN	TAJ
KILLED PAKISTANI CIVILIAN	SANAULLAH JAN
KILLED PAKISTANI CIVILIAN	RAZA KHAN
KILLED PAKISTANI CIVILIAN	JAMIL
KILLED PAKISTANI CIVILIAN	MUSTAFAA
KILLED PAKISTANI CIVILIAN	NOOR GUL
KILLED PAKISTANI CIVILIAN	JAFFAR
KILLED PAKISTANI CIVILIAN	FARAZ
KILLED PAKISTANI CIVILIAN	MUSA
KILLED PAKISTANI CIVILIAN	KAMAL
KILLED PAKISTANI CIVILIAN	NENDAR KHAN
KILLED PAKISTANI CIVILIAN	HAKIM KHAN
KILLED PAKISTANI CIVILIAN	MUSHK ALAM
KILLED PAKISTANI CIVILIAN	DARAZ KHAN
KILLED PAKISTANI CIVILIAN	MALIK DAUD KHAN
KILLED PAKISTANI CIVILIAN	ISMAIL KHAN
KILLED PAKISTANI CIVILIAN	HAJI BABAT
KILLED PAKISTANI CIVILIAN	KHNAY KHAN
KILLED PAKISTANI CIVILIAN	GUL MOHAMMED
KILLED PAKISTANI CIVILIAN	ISMAEL
KILLED PAKISTANI CIVILIAN	GUL AKBAR
KILLED PAKISTANI CIVILIAN	MOHAMMAD SHEEN
KILLED PAKISTANI CIVILIAN	LEWANAI
KILLED PAKISTANI CIVILIAN	MIR ZAMAN
KILLED PAKISTANI CIVILIAN	DIN MOHAMMAD
KILLED PAKISTANI CIVILIAN	MALIK TAREEN

KILLED PAKISTANI CIVILIAN	NOOR ALI
KILLED PAKISTANI CIVILIAN	ZARE JAN
KILLED PAKISTANI CIVILIAN	SADIQ
KILLED PAKISTANI CIVILIAN	MUSTAQEEM
KILLED PAKISTANI CIVILIAN	KHANGAI
KILLED PAKISTANI CIVILIAN	GULNAWARE
KILLED PAKISTANI CIVILIAN	FAENDA KHAN
KILLED PAKISTANI CIVILIAN	DINDAR KHAN
KILLED PAKISTANI CIVILIAN	UMARK KHAN
KILLED PAKISTANI CIVILIAN	WALI KHAN
KILLED PAKISTANI CIVILIAN	SADAR
KILLED PAKISTANI CIVILIAN	BAHKTAR
KILLED PAKISTANI CIVILIAN	MUSAMMAL KHAN
KILLED PAKISTANI CIVILIAN	SHER HAYAT KHAN
KILLED PAKISTANI CIVILIAN	NEK DAHADUR KHAN
KILLED PAKISTANI CIVILIAN	BELAL KHAN
KILLED PAKISTANI CIVILIAN	ATIF
KILLED PAKISTANI CIVILIAN	SAMAD
KILLED PAKISTANI CIVILIAN	JAMSHED
KILLED PAKISTANI CIVILIAN	DARAZ
KILLED PAKISTANI CIVILIAN	IQBAL
KILLED PAKISTANI CIVILIAN	NOOR NAWAZ
KILLED PAKISTANI CIVILIAN	YOUSAF
KILLED PAKISTANI CIVILIAN	SHAHZADA
KILLED PAKISTANI CIVILIAN	AKRAM SHAH
KILLED PAKISTANI CIVILIAN	ATIQ UR REHMAN
KILLED PAKISTANI CIVILIAN	IRSHAQ KHAN
KILLED PAKISTANI CIVILIAN	AMAR KHAN
KILLED PAKISTANI CIVILIAN	SHABBIR
KILLED PAKISTANI CIVILIAN	KALAM
KILLED PAKISTANI CIVILIAN	WAQAS
KILLED PAKISTANI CIVILIAN	BASHIR
KILLED PAKISTANI CIVILIAN	ABDUL JALIL
KILLED PAKISTANI CIVILIAN	SAEEDUR RAHMAN
KILLED PAKISTANI CIVILIAN	KHASTAR GUL
KILLED PAKISTANI CIVILIAN	MAMRUD KHAN
KILLED PAKISTANI CIVILIAN	NOORZAL KHAN
KILLED PAKISTANI CIVILIAN	TARIQ AZIZ
KILLED PAKISTANI CIVILIAN	WAHEED ULLAH
KILLED PAKISTANI CIVILIAN	MIR JAHAN GUL
KILLED PAKISTANI CIVILIAN	ALLAH MIR KHAN
KILLED PAKISTANI CIVILIAN	NOOR BHADSHAH KHAN
KILLED PAKISTANI CIVILIAN	MIR GULL JAN
KILLED PAKISTANI CIVILIAN	BATKAI JAN
KILLED PAKISTANI CIVILIAN	GALLOP HAJI JAN

KILLED PAKISTANI CIVILIAN	GULL SAID KHAN
KILLED PAKISTANI CIVILIAN	GUL DAD KHAN
KILLED PAKISTANI CIVILIAN	KHASHMIR KHAN
KILLED PAKISTANI CIVILIAN	WOLAYET KHAN
KILLED PAKISTANI CIVILIAN	SALEH KHAN
KILLED PAKISTANI CIVILIAN	SHAMROZ KHAN
KILLED PAKISTANI CIVILIAN	FAZEL REHMAN
KILLED PAKISTANI CIVILIAN	WALIULLAH
KILLED PAKISTANI CIVILIAN	SAHIBDIN
KILLED PAKISTANI CIVILIAN	MIR AJAB KHAN
KILLED PAKISTANI CIVILIAN	MIN GUL
KILLED PAKISTANI CIVILIAN	BANGAL KHAN
KILLED PAKISTANI CIVILIAN	DIL GIR KHAN
KILLED PAKISTANI CIVILIAN	SAHID DIN
KILLED PAKISTANI CIVILIAN	MIR AJAT
KILLED PAKISTANI CIVILIAN	HAQ NAWAZ
KILLED PAKISTANI CIVILIAN	HATIQULLAH
KILLED PAKISTANI CIVILIAN	AKRAM
KILLED PAKISTANI CIVILIAN	SHOAIB
KILLED PAKISTANI CIVILIAN	OSAMA HAQQANI
KILLED PAKISTANI CIVILIAN	BIBI MAMANA
KILLED PAKISTANI CIVILIAN	UZAIR
KILLED PAKISTANI CIVILIAN	SULEMAN
KILLED PAKISTANI CIVILIAN	MOHAMMED AZAM
KILLED AFGHANI CIVILIAN	NOOR MUHAMMED
KILLED AFGHANI CIVILIAN	FAMILY MEMBER OF NOOR MUHAMMED
KILLED AFGHANI CIVILIAN	FAMILY MEMBER OF NOOR MUHAMMED
KILLED AFGHANI CIVILIAN	FAMILY MEMBER OF NOOR MUHAMMED
KILLED AFGHANI CIVILIAN	FAMILY MEMBER OF NOOR MUHAMMED
KILLED AFGHANI CIVILIAN	FAMILY MEMBER OF NOOR MUHAMMED
KILLED AFGHANI CIVILIAN	FAMILY MEMBER OF NOOR MUHAMMED
KILLED AFGHANI CIVILIAN	FAMILY MEMBER OF NOOR MUHAMMED
KILLED AFGHANI CIVILIAN	FAMILY MEMBER OF NOOR MUHAMMED
KILLED AFGHANI CIVILIAN	FAMILY MEMBER OF NOOR MUHAMMED
KILLED AFGHANI CIVILIAN	FAMILY MEMBER OF NOOR MUHAMMED
KILLED AFGHANI CIVILIAN	SARDAR MUHAMMAD MAKAI
KILLED AFGHANI CIVILIAN	BILAL GULAM RASUL
KILLED AFGHANI CIVILIAN	KALED GULAM RASUL
KILLED AFGHANI CIVILIAN	SAMIN GULAM RASUL
KILLED AFGHANI CIVILIAN	WARES GULAM RASUL
KILLED AFGHANI CIVILIAN	SAKARIA RASUL
KILLED AFGHANI CIVILIAN	SAID MIR-SAID JAN
KILLED AFGHANI CIVILIAN	SAID MIR-SAID MIR
KILLED AFGHANI CIVILIAN	NAZIRA-SAID MIR
KILLED AFGHANI CIVILIAN	SOFI KASIM

KILLED AFGHANI CIVILIAN	AZIZA-KHUJA FAGIR
KILLED AFGHANI CIVILIAN	BROTHER OF HASHMATULLAH
KILLED AFGHANI CIVILIAN	NAJIBULLAH
KILLED AFGHANI CIVILIAN	ZARLASH SAID
KILLED AFGHANI CIVILIAN	IQBAL SAID
KILLED AFGHANI CIVILIAN	IMRAN SAID
KILLED AFGHANI CIVILIAN	CHILD OF IMRAN SAID
KILLED AFGHANI CIVILIAN	SHARPARI
KILLED AFGHANI CIVILIAN	AYESHA
KILLED AFGHANI CIVILIAN	JAMAL NASEER
KILLED AFGHANI CIVILIAN	ALI SAJID DAD
KILLED AFGHANI CIVILIAN	FERISHTA DAD
KILLED AFGHANI CIVILIAN	HAJI BERGET
KILLED AFGHANI CIVILIAN	SAIFULLAH
KILLED AFGHANI CIVILIAN	TAJMUHAMMED
KILLED AFGHANI CIVILIAN	CHILD OF GHULAM HAZRAT
KILLED AFGHANI CIVILIAN	CHILD OF GHULAM HAZRAT
KILLED AFGHANI CIVILIAN	NEMATULLAH HAZRAT
KILLED AFGHANI CIVILIAN	NEPHEW OF GHULAM HAZRAT
KILLED AFGHANI CIVILIAN	SON OF MULLAH OMAR
KILLED AFGHANI CIVILIAN	ABDUL SABOOR
KILLED AFGHANI CIVILIAN	GHOUHAR TAJ
KILLED AFGHANI CIVILIAN	DAUGHTER OF GHOUHAR TAJ
KILLED AFGHANI CIVILIAN	DAUGHTER OF GHOUHAR TAJ
KILLED AFGHANI CIVILIAN	DAUGHTER OF GHOUHAR TAJ
KILLED AFGHANI CIVILIAN	FAMILY MEMBER OF GHOUHAR TAJ
KILLED AFGHANI CIVILIAN	FAMILY MEMBER OF GHOUHAR TAJ
KILLED AFGHANI CIVILIAN	FAMILY MEMBER OF GHOUHAR TAJ
KILLED AFGHANI CIVILIAN	FAMILY MEMBER OF GHOUHAR TAJ
KILLED AFGHANI CIVILIAN	FAMILY MEMBER OF GHOUHAR TAJ
KILLED AFGHANI CIVILIAN	FAMILY MEMBER OF GHOUHAR TAJ
KILLED AFGHANI CIVILIAN	FAMILY MEMBER OF GHOUHAR TAJ
KILLED AFGHANI CIVILIAN	FAMILY MEMBER OF GHOUHAR TAJ
KILLED AFGHANI CIVILIAN	HUSBAND OF MUSTAFA JAN
KILLED AFGHANI CIVILIAN	GHULAM SHAH
KILLED AFGHANI CIVILIAN	FATHER OF GHULAM SHAH
KILLED AFGHANI CIVILIAN	WIFE OF GHULAM SHAH
KILLED AFGHANI CIVILIAN	CHILD OF GHULAM SHAH
KILLED AFGHANI CIVILIAN	CHILD OF GHULAM SHAH
KILLED AFGHANI CIVILIAN	CHILD OF GHULAM SHAH
KILLED AFGHANI CIVILIAN	CHILD OF GHULAM SHAH
KILLED AFGHANI CIVILIAN	RASHID
KILLED AFGHANI CIVILIAN	BROTHER OF RASHID
KILLED AFGHANI CIVILIAN	BROTHER OF RASHID
KILLED AFGHANI CIVILIAN	SISTER OF RASHID

KILLED AFGHANI CIVILIAN	SON OF MAH HASHIM
KILLED AFGHANI CIVILIAN	FAMILY MEMBER OF RAHSHID
KILLED AFGHANI CIVILIAN	FAMILY MEMBER OF RASHID
KILLED AFGHANI CIVILIAN	DARAZ KHAN
KILLED AFGHANI CIVILIAN	JEHANGIR KHAN
KILLED AFGHANI CIVILIAN	MIR AHMED
KILLED AFGHANI CIVILIAN	SIMA AHMAD
KILLED AFGHANI CIVILIAN	GUL AHMAD
KILLED AFGHANI CIVILIAN	SIDIQQA GUL AHMAD
KILLED AFGHANI CIVILIAN	SHORKRIA GUL AHMAD
KILLED AFGHANI CIVILIAN	RAZIA GUL AHMAD
KILLED AFGHANI CIVILIAN	ZAKERA GUL AHMAD
KILLED AFGHANI CIVILIAN	FAHIMA GUL AHMAD
KILLED AFGHANI CIVILIAN	RAMAZAN GUL AHMAD
KILLED AFGHANI CIVILIAN	SARDAR MAHAI
KILLED AFGHANI CIVILIAN	MEMBER OF MIZRA FAMILY
KILLED AFGHANI CIVILIAN	MEMBER OF MIZRA FAMILY
KILLED AFGHANI CIVILIAN	TORAB
KILLED AFGHANI CIVILIAN	SHABUBU
KILLED AFGHANI CIVILIAN	SAMAT
KILLED AFGHANI CIVILIAN	ABDUL
KILLED AFGHANI CIVILIAN	MARIA KHARIMI
KILLED AFGHANI CIVILIAN	AGHA MOHAMMED
KILLED AFGHANI CIVILIAN	BASHIR MOHAMMED
KILLED AFGHANI CIVILIAN	SAEED AHMAD MOHAMMED
KILLED AFGHANI CIVILIAN	HAJJI MOHAMMED
KILLED AFGHANI CIVILIAN	SALI MOHAMMED
KILLED AFGHANI CIVILIAN	FAIZAL MOHAMMED
KILLED AFGHANI CIVILIAN	WIFE OF FAIZAL MOHAMMED
KILLED AFGHANI CIVILIAN	DAUGHTER OF FAIZAL MOHAMMED
KILLED AFGHANI CIVILIAN	DAUGHTER OF FAIZAL MOHAMMED
KILLED AFGHANI CIVILIAN	SON OF FAIZAL MOHAMMED
KILLED AFGHANI CIVILIAN	BROTHER OF GULAM GILANI
KILLED AFGHANI CIVILIAN	SISTER-IN-LAW OF GULAM GILANI
KILLED AFGHANI CIVILIAN	CHILD OF GULAM GILANI
KILLED AFGHANI CIVILIAN	CHILD OF GULAM GILANI
KILLED AFGHANI CIVILIAN	SHAFI AHMAD
KILLED AFGHANI CIVILIAN	SAYA BEGUM
KILLED AFGHANI CIVILIAN	RAYHAN BEGUM
KILLED AFGHANI CIVILIAN	MUZLIFA
KILLED AFGHANI CIVILIAN	FARIGHA
KILLED AFGHANI CIVILIAN	SHERIF
KILLED AFGHANI CIVILIAN	MR. GUL
KILLED AFGHANI CIVILIAN	HAJI FAKHRAK
KILLED AFGHANI CIVILIAN	DADAN KHAN

KILLED AFGHANI CIVILIAN	PALWASHA
KILLED AFGHANI CIVILIAN	ISLAMUDIN
KILLED AFGHANI CIVILIAN	HAFIZULLAH ZAHER
KILLED AFGHANI CIVILIAN	SAEED IMRAN
KILLED AFGHANI CIVILIAN	JAVAID
KILLED AFGHANI CIVILIAN	ZAMOOR
KILLED AFGHANI CIVILIAN	HIDAYAT
KILLED AFGHANI CIVILIAN	MUSHABANA
KILLED AFGHANI CIVILIAN	KIMYA HAMID
KILLED AFGHANI CIVILIAN	SHOGOOFA
KILLED AFGHANI CIVILIAN	FEROZA
KILLED AFGHANI CIVILIAN	PARWEENAH
KILLED AFGHANI CIVILIAN	ABDUL
KILLED AFGHANI CIVILIAN	NASEER AHMAD
KILLED AFGHANI CIVILIAN	SAFIULLAH
KILLED AFGHANI CIVILIAN	MOTHER OF MUNIR
KILLED AFGHANI CIVILIAN	SISTER OF MUNIR
KILLED AFGHANI CIVILIAN	INFANT BROTHER OF MUNIR
KILLED AFGHANI CIVILIAN	ANAR GUL
KILLED AFGHANI CIVILIAN	MOTHER OF HAZIZA
KILLED AFGHANI CIVILIAN	INFANT BROTHER OF HAZIZA
KILLED AFGHANI CIVILIAN	TWELVE-YEAR-OLD GIRL
KILLED AFGHANI CIVILIAN	DAUGHTER OF ALI AWIZ
KILLED AFGHANI CIVILIAN	DAUGHTER OF ALI AWIZ
KILLED AFGHANI CIVILIAN	DAUGHTER OF ALI AWIZ
KILLED AFGHANI CIVILIAN	HUSBAND OF MAHTAB
KILLED AFGHANI CIVILIAN	CHILD OF MAHTAB
KILLED AFGHANI CIVILIAN	MOTHER-IN-LAW OF MAHTAB
KILLED AFGHANI CIVILIAN	MEMBER OF NAZIRULLAH FAMILY
KILLED AFGHANI CIVILIAN	MEMBER OF NAZIRULLAH FAMILY
KILLED AFGHANI CIVILIAN	MEMBER OF NAZIRULLAH FAMILY
KILLED AFGHANI CIVILIAN	MEMBER OF NAZIRULLAH FAMILY
KILLED AFGHANI CIVILIAN	MEMBER OF NAZIRULLAH FAMILY
KILLED AFGHANI CIVILIAN	ZARPARI ISMAIL
KILLED AFGHANI CIVILIAN	FAIZAL ISMAIL
KILLED AFGHANI CIVILIAN	FAIZAL MOHAMMED
KILLED AFGHANI CIVILIAN	SALI MOHAMMED
KILLED AFGHANI CIVILIAN	SHAH MOHAMMED
KILLED AFGHANI CIVILIAN	FAMILY MEMBER OF SHAH MOHAMMED
KILLED AFGHANI CIVILIAN	FAMILY MEMBER OF SHAH MOHAMMED
KILLED AFGHANI CIVILIAN	FAMILY MEMBER OF SHAH MOHAMMED
KILLED AFGHANI CIVILIAN	FAMILY MEMBER OF SHAH MOHAMMED
KILLED AFGHANI CIVILIAN	FAMILY MEMBER OF SHAH MOHAMMED
KILLED AFGHANI CIVILIAN	FAMILY MEMBER OF SHAH MOHAMMED
KILLED AFGHANI CIVILIAN	FAMILY MEMBER OF SHAH MOHAMMED

KILLED AFGHANI CIVILIAN	FAMILY MEMBER OF SHAH MOHAMMED
KILLED AFGHANI CIVILIAN	FAMILY MEMBER OF SHAH MOHAMMED
KILLED AFGHANI CIVILIAN	FAMILY MEMBER OF SHAH MOHAMMED
KILLED AFGHANI CIVILIAN	FAMILY MEMBER OF SHAH MOHAMMED
KILLED AFGHANI CIVILIAN	FAMILY MEMBER OF SHAH MOHAMMED
KILLED AFGHANI CIVILIAN	FAMILY MEMBER OF SHAH MOHAMMED
KILLED AFGHANI CIVILIAN	FAMILY MEMBER OF SHAH MOHAMMED
KILLED AFGHANI CIVILIAN	FAMILY MEMBER OF SHAH MOHAMMED
KILLED AFGHANI CIVILIAN	FAMILY MEMBER OF SHAH MOHAMMED
KILLED AFGHANI CIVILIAN	MOTHER OF NIK MOHAMMED
KILLED AFGHANI CIVILIAN	FATHER OF NIK MOHAMMED
KILLED AFGHANI CIVILIAN	NIECE OF NIK MOHAMMED
KILLED AFGHANI CIVILIAN	SISTER-IN-LAW OF NIK MOHAMMED
KILLED AFGHANI CIVILIAN	ALI SAJIB
KILLED AFGHANI CIVILIAN	FERISHTA
KILLED AFGHANI CIVILIAN	FAMILY MEMBER OF ABDUL BAQ
KILLED AFGHANI CIVILIAN	FAMILY MEMBER OF ABDUL BAQ
KILLED AFGHANI CIVILIAN	MIRA JAN
KILLED AFGHANI CIVILIAN	LAL MUHAMMAD
KILLED AFGHANI CIVILIAN	MOHIBULLAH
KILLED AFGHANI CIVILIAN	SHER MUHAMMAD
KILLED AFGHANI CIVILIAN	BIBI GUL
KILLED AFGHANI CIVILIAN	HAKIMULLAH KHAN
KILLED AFGHANI CIVILIAN	HAMZA KHAN
KILLED AFGHANI CIVILIAN	CHILD OF JUMA KHAN
KILLED AFGHANI CIVILIAN	CHILD OF JUMA KHAN
KILLED AFGHANI CIVILIAN	CHILD OF JUMA KHAN
KILLED AFGHANI CIVILIAN	CHILD OF JUMA KHAN
KILLED AFGHANI CIVILIAN	CHILD OF JUMA KHAN
KILLED AFGHANI CIVILIAN	ABDUL QADIR
KILLED AFGHANI CIVILIAN	AGHA PEDAR
KILLED AFGHANI CIVILIAN	DAUGHTER OF PEDAR
KILLED AFGHANI CIVILIAN	SON OF PEDAR
KILLED AFGHANI CIVILIAN	NEIGHBOR OF PEDAR
KILLED AFGHANI CIVILIAN	DARYA KHAN MALIKSHAI WAZIR
KILLED AFGHANI CIVILIAN	SATIK
KILLED AFGHANI CIVILIAN	TURIAL
KILLED AFGHANI CIVILIAN	PARDES
KILLED AFGHANI CIVILIAN	WIFE OF ABDUL RASOOL
KILLED AFGHANI CIVILIAN	MOTHER OF ALAM GUL
KILLED AFGHANI CIVILIAN	FATHER OF ALAM GUL
KILLED AFGHANI CIVILIAN	BROTHER OF ALAM GUL
KILLED AFGHANI CIVILIAN	BROTHER OF ALAM GUL
KILLED AFGHANI CIVILIAN	BROTHER OF ALAM GUL
KILLED AFGHANI CIVILIAN	BROTHER OF ALAM GUL

KILLED AFGHANI CIVILIAN	SISTER OF ALAM GUL
KILLED AFGHANI CIVILIAN	SISTER OF ALAM GUL
KILLED AFGHANI CIVILIAN	HAJI GHAN
KILLED AFGHANI CIVILIAN	FAMILY MEMBER OF HAJI GHAN
KILLED AFGHANI CIVILIAN	FAMILY MEMBER OF HAJI GHAN
KILLED AFGHANI CIVILIAN	FAMILY MEMBER OF HAJI GHAN
KILLED AFGHANI CIVILIAN	FAMILY MEMBER OF HAJI GHAN
KILLED AFGHANI CIVILIAN	FAMILY MEMBER OF HAJI GHAN
KILLED AFGHANI CIVILIAN	FAMILY MEMBER OF HAJI GHAN
KILLED AFGHANI CIVILIAN	FAMILY MEMBER OF HAJI GHAN
KILLED AFGHANI CIVILIAN	FAMILY MEMBER OF HAJI GHAN
KILLED AFGHANI CIVILIAN	FAMILY MEMBER OF HAJI GHAN
KILLED AFGHANI CIVILIAN	FAMILY MEMBER OF HAJI GHAN
KILLED AFGHANI CIVILIAN	FAMILY MEMBER OF HAJI GHAN

NOTES

This novel takes its name, water & power, from a Cold War Kids song of the same name, from their 2013 album *Dear Miss Lonely Hearts.*

All images are Property of the Author, except when noted in text or below.

"Subject #00215" was written by Jaime Fountaine, an author based in Philadelphia, PA.

"Brief History: Taillhook Scandal": Information derived from PBS Frontline Online and the following:

> "a lot of female Navy pilots are go-go dancers..." Healy, Melissa. "Pentagon Blasts Tailhook Probe, Two Admirals Resign". *Los Angeles Times* (September 25, 1992).

> "do another report..." William H. McMichael. *The Mother of All Hooks: The Story of the U.S. Navy's Tailhook Scandal* (Transaction Publishers, 1997), p. 273

> "sound bite, bumper sticker approach" Rear Adm. Kendell Pease, the Chief of Navy Information, quoted in *New York Times* article "Navy Defines Sexual Harassment With the Colors of Traffic Lights." (June, 19, 1993)

The Urdu text in "Participation #24780" was written by Masroor Hussain in response to the English text I wrote. There is no translation. My decision to include an untranslated non-English script was inspired by Myung Mi Kim's *Commons.*

"Case Report: Dirge" was inspired by Myung Mi Kim's *Commons.* The details of the bombings in that same section are derived from The Bureau of Investigative Journalism's website tab Naming The Dead, under Case Studies. https://v1.thebureauinvestigates.com/namingthedead/?lang=en

Family names and Country names of killed civilians in "Cast: In Order of Disappearance" are also derived from The Bureau of Investigative Journalism.

ACKNOWLEDGEMENTS

This novel is indebted to Ari Folman's 2008 film *Waltz With Bashir*, which changed the way I viewed military literature.

Thank you to everyone I interviewed. I know we agreed that it was best to remain anonymous, but I just want to publicly acknowledge that most of this book is made up of y'all's words. You know who you are.

Our writing group (my muthafuckin' people!): Alex Benke, Arielle Roberts, Ben Dreith, Brian Lupo, Camilla Sterne, Leah Scott, Madi Chamberlain, Patrick Krause, Tucker Jameson, and Thuyanh Astbury, who read, revised, arranged, and encouraged this book in all its forms over the years. This book wouldn't be shit without y'all's sharpness and care.

Thank you to Jenn Ashworth, Joe Cooper, Lorenzo James, and Katie Jean Shinkle for reading and giving tons of helpful feedback that changed the course of the final manuscript.

As always, thank you to my wife Tara, and daughter Jada, for all types of logistical, emotional, and financial support so that I am able to write. And thank you for reading my stuff when I ask.

Khadijah Queen and Nikki Wallschlaeger, y'all killed the blurbs for this book, and I'm still fanboying that two of my favorite poets wrote such wonderful things. Right on, jack!

Thank you to the following journals who published excerpts of this novel: *Connotations Press*, *Rigorous Journal*, *Tethered by Letters*, and *Granta*.

And a huge shout out to Tarpaulin Sky Press for believing in this book and doing the hard work to get it printed and out into the wild.

ABOUT THE AUTHOR

Shortlisted for *Granta's* "Best of Young American Novelists," Steven Dunn is the author of the novel *Potted Meat* (Tarpaulin Sky, 2016), which was co-winner of the Tarpaulin Sky Book Prize and a finalist for a Colorado Book Award. He was born and raised in West Virginia, and after ten years in the Navy he earned a B.A. in Creative Writing from University of Denver. He is currently a MFA candidate at Goddard College. His work can be found in *Rigorous, Blink Ink, Best Small Fictions 2018, Columbia Journal*, and *Granta*.

TARPAULIN SKY PRESS

Warped from one world to another. (*THE NATION*) Somewhere between Artaud and Lars Von Trier. (*VICE*) Hallucinatory ... trance-inducing.... A kind of nut job's notebook.... Breakneck prose harnesses the throbbing pulse of language itself.... Playful, experimental appeal.... Multivalent, genre-bending.... Unrelenting, grotesque beauty. (*PUBLISHERS WEEKLY*) Simultaneously metaphysical and visceral.... Scary, sexual, and intellectually disarming. (*HUFFINGTON POST*) Horrifying and humbling.... (*THE RUMPUS*) Wholly new. (*IOWA REVIEW*) ....only becomes more surreal. (*NPR BOOKS*) The opposite of boring.... An ominous conflagration devouring the bland terrain of conventional realism.... Dangerous language, a murderous kind ... discomfiting, filthy, hilarious, and ecstatic. (*BOOKSLUT*) Creating a zone where elegance and grace can gambol with the just-plain-fucked-up. (*HTML GIANT*) Uncomfortably enjoyable. (*AMERICAN BOOK REVIEW*) Consistently inventive. (*TRIQUARTERLY*) A peculiar, personal music that is at once apart from and very much surrounded by the world. (*VERSE*) A world of wounded voices. (*HYPERALLERGIC*) Futile, sad, and beautiful. (*NEWPAGES*) Inspired and unexpected. Highly recommended. (*AFTER ELLEN*)

MORE FROM TS PRESS >>

JENNIFER S. CHENG
MOON: LETTERS, MAPS, POEMS

Co-winner, Tarpaulin Sky Book Award, chosen by Bhanu Kapil
Publishers Weekly, Starred Review
SPD Poetry Bestseller
Nominated for the PEN American Open Book Award

Mixing fable and fact, extraordinary and ordinary, Jennifer S. Cheng's hybrid collection, *Moon: Letters, Maps, Poems*, draws on various Chinese mythologies about women, particularly that of Chang'E (the Lady in the Moon), uncovering the shadow stories of our myths. "Exhilarating ... An alt-epic for the 21st century ... Visionary ... Rich and glorious." (**PUBLISHERS WEEKLY STARRED REVIEW**) "If reading is a form of pilgrimage, then Cheng gives us its charnel ground events, animal conversions, guiding figures and elemental life." (**BHANU KAPIL**) "Each of the voices in Jennifer S. Cheng's *Moon* speaks as if she's 'the last girl on earth.' ... With curiosity and attention, *Moon* shines its light on inquiry as art, asking as making. In the tradition of Fanny Howe's poetics of bewilderment, Cheng gives us a poetics of possibility." (**JENNIFER TSENG**) "Cheng's newest poetry collection bravely tests language and the beautiful boundaries of body and geography ... A rich and deeply satisfying read." (**AIMEE NEZHUKUMATATHIL**)

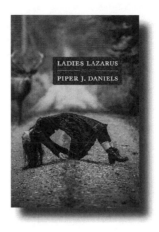

PIPER J. DANIELS
LADIES LAZARUS

Co-winner, Tarpaulin Sky Book Award
Nominated for the PEN/Diamonstein-Spielvogel Award
for the Art of the Essay

Equal parts séance, polemic, and love letter, Piper J. Daniels's *Ladies Lazarus* examines evangelical upbringing, sexual trauma, queer identity, and mental illness with a raw intensity that moves between venom and grace. Fueled by wanderlust, Daniels travels the country, unearthing the voices of forgotten women. Girls and ghosts speak freely, murdered women serve as mentors, and those who've languished in unmarked graves convert their names to psalms. At every turn, Daniels invites the reader to engage, not in the soothing narrative of healing, but in the literal and metaphorical dynamism of death and resurrection. "Beautifully written collection of 11 lyric essays ... Daniels emerges as an empowering and noteworthy voice." (*PUBLISHERS WEEKLY*) "*Ladies Lazarus* is the best debut I've read in a long time. Daniels has resurrected the personal essay and what it is and what it can do." (**JENNY BOULLY**) "An extremely intelligent, impressively understated, and achingly powerful work." (**DAVID SHIELDS**) "A siren song from planet woman, a love letter from the body, a resistance narrative against the dark." (**LIDIA YUKNAVITCH**)

STEVEN DUNN
POTTED MEAT

Co-winner, Tarpaulin Sky Book Award
Shortlist, *Granta*'s "Best of Young American Novelists"
Finalist, Colorado Book Award
SPD Fiction Bestseller

Set in a decaying town in West Virginia, Steven Dunn's debut novel, *Potted Meat,* follows a boy into adolescence as he struggles with abuse, poverty, alcoholism, and racial tensions. A meditation on trauma and the ways in which a person might surivive, if not thrive, *Potted Meat* examines the fear, power, and vulnerability of storytelling itself. "101 pages of miniature texts that keep tapping the nails in, over and over, while speaking as clearly and directly as you could ask.... Bone Thugs, underage drinking, alienation, death, love, Bob Ross, dreams of blood.... Flooded with power." (**BLAKE BUTLER,** *VICE MAGAZINE*) "Full of wonder and silence and beauty and strangeness and ugliness and sadness.... This book needs to be read." (**LAIRD HUNT**) "A visceral intervention across the surface of language, simultaneously cutting to its depths, to change the world.... I feel grateful to be alive during the time in which Steven Dunn writes books." (**SELAH SATERSTROM**)

ELIZABETH HALL
I HAVE DEVOTED MY LIFE TO THE CLITORIS

Co-winner, Tarpaulin Sky Book Award
Finalist, Lambda Literary Award for Bisexual Nonfiction
SPD Nonfiction Bestseller

Debut author Elizabeth Hall set out to read everything that has been written about the clitoris. The result is "Freud, terra cotta cunts, hyenas, anatomists, and Acker, mixed with a certain slant of light on a windowsill and a leg thrown open invite us. Bawdy and beautiful." (**WENDY C. ORTIZ**). "An orgy of information ... rendered with graceful care, delivering in small bites an investigation of the clit that is simultaneously a meditation on the myriad ways in which smallness hides power." (***THE RUMPUS***) "Marvelously researched and sculpted.... bulleted points rat-tat-tatting the patriarchy, strobing with pleasure." (**DODIE BELLAMY**) "Philosophers and theorists have always asked what the body is—Hall just goes further than the classical ideal of the male body, beyond the woman as a vessel or victim, past genre as gender, to the clitoris. And we should follow her." (***KENYON REVIEW***) "Gorgeous little book about a gorgeous little organ.... The 'tender button' finally gets its due." (**JANET SARBANES**) "You will learn and laugh .... God this book is glorious." (**SUZANNE SCANLON**)

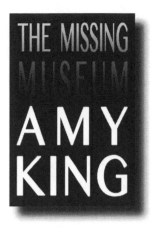

AMY KING
THE MISSING MUSEUM

Co-winner, Tarpaulin Sky Book Award
SPD Poetry Bestseller

Nothing that is complicated may ever be simplified, but rather catalogued, cherished, exposed. *The Missing Museum* spans art, physics & the spiritual, including poems that converse with the sublime and ethereal. They act through ekphrasis, apostrophe & alchemical conjuring. They amass, pile, and occasionally flatten as matter is beaten into text. Here is a kind of directory of the world as it rushes into extinction, in order to preserve and transform it at once. "'Understanding' is not a part of the book's project, but rather a condition that one must move through like a person hurriedly moving through a museum." (*PUBLISHERS WEEKLY*) "Women's National Book Association Award-winner Amy King balances passages that can prompt head-scratching wonder with a direct fusillade of shouty caps.... You're not just seeing through her eyes but, perhaps more importantly, breathing through her lungs." (*LAMBDA LITERARY*) "A visceral stunner ... and an instruction manual.... King's archival work testifies to the power—however obscured by the daily noise of our historical moment—of art, of the possibility for artists to legislate the world." (*KENYON REVIEW*)

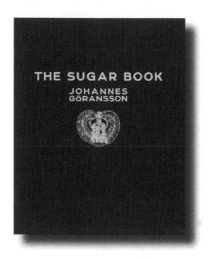

JOHANNES GÖRANSSON
THE SUGAR BOOK

SPD Poetry Bestseller

Johannes Göransson's *The Sugar Book* marks the author's third title with TS Press, following his acclaimed *Haute Surveillance* and *entrance to a colonial pageant in which we all begin to intricate.* "Doubling down on his trademark misanthropic imagery amid a pageantry of the unpleasant, Johannes Göransson strolls through a violent Los Angeles in this hybrid of prose and verse.... The motifs are plentiful and varied ... pubic hair, Orpheus, law, pigs, disease, Francesca Woodman ... and the speaker's hunger for cocaine and copulation..... Fans of Göransson's distorted poetics will find this a productive addition to his body of work". (*PUBLISHERS WEEKLY*) "Sends its message like a mail train. Visceral Surrealism. His end game is an exit wound." (*FANZINE*) "As savagely anti-idealist as Burroughs or Guyotat or Ballard. Like those writers, he has no interest in assuring the reader that she or he lives, along with the poet, on the right side of history." (*ENTROPY MAGAZINE*) "Convulses wildly like an animal that has eaten the poem's interior and exterior all together with silver." (**KIM HYESOON**) "'I make a language out of the bleed-through.' Göransson sure as fuck does. These poems made me cry. So sad and anxious and genius and glary bright." (**REBECCA LOUDON**)

AARON APPS
INTERSEX

"Favorite Nonfiction of 2015," Dennis Cooper
SPD Bestseller and Staff Pick

Intersexed author Aaron Apps's hybrid-genre memoir adopts and upends historical descriptors of hermaphroditic bodies such as "imposter," "sexual pervert," "freak of nature," and "unfortunate monstrosity," tracing the author's own monstrous sex as it perversely intertwines with gender expectations and medical discourse. "Graphic vignettes involving live alligators, diarrhea in department store bathrooms, domesticity, dissected animals, and the medicalization of sex.... Unafraid of failure and therefore willing to employ risk as a model for confronting violence, living with it, learning from it." (*AMERICAN BOOK REVIEW*) "I felt this book in the middle of my own body. Like the best kind of memoir, Apps brings a reader close to an experience of life that is both 'unattainable' and attentive to 'what will emerge from things.' In doing so, he has written a book that bursts from its very frame." (**BHANU KAPIL**)

Excerpts from *Intersex* were nominated for a Pushcart Prize by *Carolina Quarterly*, and appear in *Best American Essays 2014*.

CLAIRE DONATO
BURIAL

A debut novella that slays even seasoned readers. Set in the mind of a narrator who is grieving the loss of her father, who conflates her hotel room with the morgue, and who encounters characters that may not exist, *Burial* is a little story about an immeasurable black hole; an elegy in prose at once lyrical and intelligent, with no small amount of rot and vomit and ghosts. "Poetic, trance-inducing language turns a reckoning with the confusion of mortality into readerly joy at the sensuality of living." (*PUBLISHERS WEEKLY* "BEST SUMMER READS") "A dark, multivalent, genre-bending book.... Unrelenting, grotesque beauty an exhaustive recursive obsession about the unburiability of the dead, and the incomprehensibility of death." (*PUBLISHERS WEEKLY* STARRED REVIEW) "Dense, potent language captures that sense of the unreal that, for a time, pulls people in mourning to feel closer to the dead than the living.... Sartlingly original and effective." (*MINNEAPOLIS STAR-TRIBUNE*) "A grief-dream, an attempt to un-sew pain from experience and to reveal it in language." (*HTML GIANT*) "A full and vibrant illustration of the restless turns of a mind undergoing trauma.... Donato makes and unmakes the world with words, and what is left shimmers with pain and delight." (BRIAN EVENSON) "A gorgeous fugue, an unforgettable progression, a telling I cannot shake." (HEATHER CHRISTLE) "Claire Donato's assured and poetic debut augurs a promising career." (BENJAMIN MOSER)

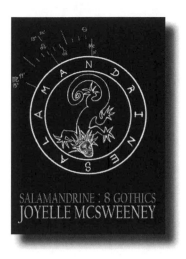

JOYELLE MCSWEENEY
SALAMANDRINE: 8 GOTHICS

Following poet and playwright Joyelle McSweeney's acclaimed novels *Flet*, from Fence Books, and *Nylund, The Sarcographer*, from Tarpaulin Sky Press, comes a collection of shorter prose texts by McSweeney, *Salamandrine: 8 Gothics*, perhaps better described as a series of formal/ generic lenses refracting the dread and isolation of contemporary life and producing a distorted, attenuated, spasmatic experience of time, as accompanies motherhood. "Vertiginous.... Denying the reader any orienting poles for the projected reality.... McSweeney's breakneck prose harnesses the throbbing pulse of language itself." (*PUBLISHERS WEEKLY*) "Biological, morbid, fanatic, surreal, McSweeney's impulses are to go to the rhetoric of the maternity mythos by evoking the spooky, sinuous syntaxes of the gothic and the cleverly constructed political allegory. At its core is the proposition that writing the mother-body is a viscid cage match with language and politics in a declining age.... This collection is the sexy teleological apocrypha of motherhood literature, a siren song for those mothers 'with no soul to photograph.'" (*THE BROOKLYN RAIL*) "Language commits incest with itself.... Sounds repeat, replicate, and mutate in her sentences, monstrous sentences of aural inbreeding and consangeous consonants, strung out and spinning like the dirtiest double-helix, dizzy with disease...." (*QUARTERLY WEST*)

JENNY BOULLY
NOT MERELY BECAUSE OF THE UNKNOWN THAT WAS STALKING TOWARD THEM

"This is undoubtedly the contemporary re-treatment that Peter Pan deserves.... Simultaneously metaphysical and visceral, these addresses from Wendy to Peter in lyric prose are scary, sexual, and intellectually disarming." (*HUFFINGTON POST*) In her second SPD Bestseller from Tarpaulin Sky Press, *not merely because of the unknown that was stalking toward them*, Jenny Boully presents a "deliciously creepy" swan song from Wendy Darling to Peter Pan, as Boully reads between the lines of J. M. Barrie's *Peter and Wendy* and emerges with the darker underside, with sinister and subversive places. *not merely because of the unknown* explores, in dreamy and dark prose, how we love, how we pine away, and how we never stop loving and pining away. "To delve into Boully's work is to dive with faith from the plank — to jump, with hope and belief and a wish to see what the author has given us: a fresh, imaginative look at a tale as ageless as Peter himself." (*BOOKSLUT*) "Jenny Boully is a deeply weird writer—in the best way." (**ANDER MONSON**)

MORE FICTION, NONFICTION, POETRY & HYBRID TEXTS FROM TARPAULIN SKY PRESS

FULL-LENGTH BOOKS

Jenny Boully, *[one love affair]**

Ana Božičević, *Stars of the Night Commute*

Traci O. Connor, *Recipes for Endangered Species*

Mark Cunningham, *Body Language*

Danielle Dutton, *Attempts at a Life*

Sarah Goldstein, *Fables*

Johannes Göransson, *Entrance to a colonial pageant in which we all begin to intricate*

Johannes Göransson, *Haute Surveillance*

Noah Eli Gordon & Joshua Marie Wilkinson, *Figures for a Darkroom Voice*

Dana Green, *Sometimes the Air in the Room Goes Missing*

Gordon Massman, *The Essential Numbers 1991 - 2008*

Joyelle McSweeney, *Nylund, The Sarcographer*

Kim Parko, *The Grotesque Child*

Joanna Ruocco, *Man's Companions*

Kim Gek Lin Short, *The Bugging Watch & Other Exhibits*

Kim Gek Lin Short, *China Cowboy*

Shelly Taylor, *Black-Eyed Heifer*

Max Winter, *The Pictures*

David Wolach, *Hospitalogy*

Andrew Zornoza, *Where I Stay*

CHAPBOOKS

Sandy Florian, *32 Pedals and 47 Stops*
James Haug, *Scratch*
Claire Hero, *Dollyland*
Paula Koneazny, *Installation*
Paul McCormick, *The Exotic Moods of Les Baxter*
Teresa K. Miller, *Forever No Lo*
Jeanne Morel, *That Crossing Is Not Automatic*
Andrew Michael Roberts, *Give Up*
Brandon Shimoda, *The Inland Sea*
Chad Sweeney, *A Mirror to Shatter the Hammer*
Emily Toder, *Brushes With*

G.C. Waldrep, *One Way No Exit*

Tarpaulin Sky Literary Journal
in print and online

tarpaulinsky.com